Even creatures of the night need love.

Are you afraid of the dark? Maybe you just need a friendly guiding hand. Be brave and explore these lustful tales of supernatural love. Your heart will race and you'll shiver in anticipation as you discover that sometimes very good things go bump in the night.

Scared Stiff
Copyright©2017 Jimi Goninan
ISBN 978-1-911478-23-2
Cover art and design by Dawné Dominique

Published by
Lydian Press 2017
Find us on the World Wide Web at
http://www.lydianpress.com

CONTENTS

SCARED STIFF

JIMI GONINAN

Lydian Press

DEDICATION

For Ella, My enduring Halloween Queen…

DEVIL MAY CARE

Gabriel Dieudonné stirred in his king-sized bed, before blearily opening his eyes. Stretching out, he relished the feel of the red satin sheets sliding against his naked skin. As he turned over, Gabriel expected to come into contact with his husband's powerfully built form, but realized that he was alone in the bed when his hands encountered nothing but air.

Where did he get to this morning?

His body still ached in a pleasant reminder of the exquisite torture he'd received at the hands of his Lord and Master – as his husband affectionately liked to be called – the night before. His ass had taken the brunt of the punishment, being ridden for hours without mercy…not that Gabriel ever complained. Squeezing his ass muscles together, he got an agreeable reminder of a job well done. The temperature in the room was satisfyingly warm, as always, and the air felt thick with just the merest chemical hint about it – it was reassuringly familiar.

Throwing off the sheet, Gabriel looked up at his reflection in the mirrored ceiling – his husband's decorating tastes – and was satisfied with what he saw.

Vanity, thy name is Gabriel.

In his defense, Gabriel was quite a sight to behold. His smooth body was bronzed and honed to perfection, and his tousled dirty blond hair and cornflower blue eyes made for an arresting combination. His manhood was erect and at its full eight inches, as was usually the case when he awoke of a morning. Indeed, he was in the best shape of his life and looked far younger than his true age – a closely guarded secret.

Getting out of bed, Gabriel walked over to the window and threw back the heavy black velvet curtains, which allowed a warm red light to spill into the room. It was a view he'd grown quite fond of over the years, although he knew others often found it rather unpleasant. Looking out, he could see the ochre-colored rock walls of a seemingly bottomless crevasse. Along the sides, a multitude of doors ran in a series of lines, each belonging to a cell. The number of cells increased on a daily basis, as an unending stream of new prisoners came from above. Behind each door, laid a personally-tailored, private hell. Constant cries of misery, blended together into a white noise of anguish and despair that was barely audible through the thickness of the glass.

When he'd first arrived, Gabriel was stunned by just who'd qualified for eternal damnation. Naturally, there was an over-abundance of lawyers and politicians, but far from being the domain of sodomites and whores, the place was populated with *fine upstanding people* with nasty secrets. All of them well-deserving of the punishment they were to receive for time without end, although the memory of their treatment was erased on a regular basis and restarted, as human minds tended to come apart after a decade or so of unrelenting suffering.

Sighing, Gabriel absentmindedly twirled his heavy platinum wedding ring about his finger.

Now, where on earth is my husband?

It wasn't always easy being married to the Devil.

* * *

Truthfully, it had come as something of a surprise to Gabriel that he'd actually ended up in Hell – mostly because he'd convinced himself that it didn't exist. Even though Reverend Solomon Jones, the fiery preacher of Gabriel's hometown, had done his level best to persuade him, and the rest of his congregation, otherwise. The preacher was very much of the fire and brimstone ilk, apparently convinced that without his stern moral guidance, everyone was going to Hell, in particular, those men who committed the most egregious sin of all – loving another man.

"Sodomites shall burn for all eternity, their putrid flesh melting from their bones, their torment never-ending," thundered Reverend Jones, at least once a week.

His Sunday school sermons were even more disturbing, given that they were delivered directly to children. Growing up, it'd been Gabriel's most dreaded time of the week, being terrorized straight after church, for a full one and a half hours. To make matters worse, Reverend Jones was rather liberal with the use of his long wooden cane, which he used to rap the hands and buttocks of those children he deemed sinful that week...it was rare that anybody escaped his attention for long.

I don't see why God wants him to hurt children. Sometimes it seems as if he kinda enjoys it.

Gabriel received more than a handful of cruel blows from the cane during his childhood, as did the majority of his friends and classmates. Thankfully, that had ended in his mid-teens, once attendance became optional.

During his time in the small Midwest town of Chestnut Hollow, Gabriel had successfully kept his forbidden desires well hidden. Confining it to furtive masturbation fantasies late at night when his parents were fast asleep. It wasn't that he had no attraction to women, indeed, he'd even had a few wet dreams about some of the cheerleaders, but his carnal yearnings were much stronger toward the male of the species. One specimen in particular caught his attention early on – Andrew Madison, the captain of the football team and the object of lust for a good many of his peers. He was the very picture of the All-American boy next door with chestnut curls, green eyes and a killer smile. Gabriel had lost count of how many times he'd spilt his seed thinking of what he and the strapping footballer might get up to in the locker room after a big game. In fact, it was the only reason that Gabriel had bothered attending the games, although he and Andrew had barely ever had a conversation.

To his great relief, no one appeared to suspect Gabriel's true nature, but that didn't stop the good reverend from paying Gabriel a special visit before his departure and haranguing him for over two hours on the evils of city life.

4

"They're full of degenerates, criminals and whores, all there to tempt you into their perverted ways," lectured Reverend Jones. "They'll turn even the most clean-living, god-fearing man into a depraved abomination. Personally, I think your parents are damned fools for allowing you to leave. May God have mercy on your soul."

As if I didn't already feel guilty enough.

It was fortunate indeed that his parents were more open-minded than the preacher, both having travelled outside into the big, bright world; before they'd settled down to have a family. It helped that his father's family hailed from France a few generations back, so traveling was in their blood. To be fair, there wasn't much of a future in Chestnut Hollow for anyone not agriculturally minded.

"You take care now, son," counseled his father, Patrick, an older-looking version of Gabriel with the start of a middle-age spread. "Remember, we're always here if you need us."

"Make us proud, my darling boy," said his mother, Roberta, a kind-featured buxom woman, with a beautiful mane of auburn tresses. "I just know you're going to be a star!"

With his parents' blessing, Gabriel had left as soon as he was of age and moved to New York with stars in his eyes. He was something of a timid lad as a child, but once Gabriel took to the stage he discovered that he could lose himself in the different characters and his insecurities fell away. For the first time he felt noticed and truly alive. Of course, he often reverted back to his shy state when out of the spotlight.

By the end of high school, he'd managed to come out of his shell and had grown quite popular. Even Andrew had a smile and a wave for him on occasion, although unlike an uplifting teen film there was no magic moment when the broad-shouldered quarterback realized that Gabriel was the love of his life and they ran off happily together. Instead, Andrew knocked up his cheerleader girlfriend, Sandy, and a hasty marriage ensued just after graduation.

So much for that, then.

Gabriel left soon afterwards, his head full of dreams and his heart full of hope. Unfortunately, things didn't work out quite as planned. While he'd been the star of high school and community theatre productions, once in the big city, Gabriel soon found that he was just one of many desperate for fame and fortune. After graduating from the drama program at the University of Columbia, he was bursting with expectation and pluck. Sadly, years of auditions that tended to go nowhere meant that his part-time job waiting tables slowly became his profession. The only success he'd had was a small role with a touring company production of Macbeth. It'd lasted about four months and was generally well attended but nothing more had come of it.

In his darker moments, Gabriel thought about giving up on his aspirations and returning home to Chestnut Hollow, but that felt like a failure he couldn't face. Besides, he knew in his heart that a small-town life would be the end of him.

A fate worse than death.

At a loss and unsure of which path he should take, Gabriel couldn't see a way forward. Of course, that was before he'd met Lucifer.

* * *

It was late in the afternoon on a rainy October day and Gabriel was feeling rather sorry for himself. He'd worked the morning shift at Mona's, a restaurant near his apartment in Chinatown, and barely received any tips. Then he'd gotten a call from his agent, Shelley Diamond. A formidable woman in her mid-sixties with friendly violet eyes and a wild array of curly, bright-purple hair, she had been the only agent willing to give Gabriel a shot.

"Sorry, Doll," said Shelley in her customary gravelly voice. "You didn't get the job."

I can't even get a commercial to sell toilet paper! What the fuck is wrong with me?

"Thanks for letting me know, Shelley."

"Chin up! You never know when you'll get your break."

Is this how I want to live the rest of my life? Desperately hoping to get any acting job? I live in a tiny, crappy apartment. I haven't been able to afford new clothes in nearly two years and if it weren't for the restaurant leftovers I'd probably starve. Why couldn't I have wanted to be a damn farmer?

He'd been planning on spending the night in, wrapped up in blankets on the sofa and drowning his sorrows in an orgy of cookie dough ice cream and reality TV, but his best friend and flat mate, Trisha Monroe, had other ideas. She was a stick-thin bundle of energy in her early twenties, with dark smoky eyes and a shock of electric blue hair, looking every inch the fashion intern. Rather fitting, seeing she worked at the prestigious fashion magazine, Gazelle.

"Oh, no you don't!" declared Trisha, upon returning home and seeing Gabriel set up in full pity mode on the sofa.

"Don't what?" muttered Gabriel, burying himself further under the blankets.

"You're not staying home and moping. We're going out!"

"How? You're as broke as I am?" lamented Gabriel. "Anyway, I really don't feel like it."

"That's exactly why we need to go. We did a photo shoot in this funky bar yesterday and one of the bartenders, this really gorgeous guy, Trevor, said to come back any time I wanted free drinks."

"I bet he did," smirked Gabriel.

Gabriel had borne witness to Trisha's almost supernatural ability to get guys to do what she wanted. Why she hadn't used this ability to find them a much better apartment Gabriel didn't know.

"So, get your sorry ass off of that sofa and get dressed."

I really don't want to go. Why can't she just let me be miserable in peace? How can I get out of this?

"I have nothing to wear," bemoaned Gabriel, hoping that she might relent.

Without a further word, Trisha disappeared into Gabriel's closet-sized bedroom and rummaged around for a few minutes before emerging triumphant, holding a pair of naturally distressed jeans and a pair of black dress shoes with Cuban heels he hadn't worn for years.

"Let me see if I still have it," mumbled Trisha as she began to rifle through her own wardrobe. "Perfect!"

In her hands was a fitted, cobalt blue shirt that had been left behind by one of her many paramours.

"OK, now you can get dressed," proclaimed Trisha with great glee. "We're going down to Hades!"

"We're what now?"

"Hades. It's the name of the bar."

Reverend Jones was right, after all.

Under duress, Gabriel left his sofa fortress and dressed in the outfit that Trisha had put together. Looking in the mirror, he had to admit that she certainly had a good eye.

Two hours later, Gabriel was pleasantly buzzed after barely two drinks. Trevor's desire to impress Trisha had led to some very generous free pouring. Gabriel doubted he'd even need another drink to make it through the night.

Trisha was right. This is better than sulking at home.

He was currently sitting by himself, Trevor and Trisha having disappeared ten minutes earlier. Not that he blamed her in the slightest; Trevor was a drop-dead gorgeous Brazilian, with chiseled features and smooth, mocha-colored skin. Looking around, Gabriel was enamored by the ambiance of the bar. It had a warm, yet dangerous, appeal. It was spacious and open but still gave the impression of intimacy with muted red lighting and plush black leather sofas tucked into corners. It seemed the type of bar where all manner of debauchery could be had.

Suddenly, a dark and handsome stranger with rakishly disheveled raven hair and beguiling emerald eyes appeared by his side. Dressed in a perfectly tailored black suit and a crisp white shirt unbuttoned at the collar, the stranger exuded sex appeal.

"Devil's Nipple?" offered the man.

He didn't say what I thought he did, right?

"Sorry?"

"Devil's Nipple, it's the best cocktail they make here. Ever so tasty. Would you like one?"

"Sure, why not?"

The stranger merely nodded at the ruggedly attractive, Nordic God who had replaced Trevor, and two vibrant-red drinks were soon set before them.

Do they only employ models here? If he's buying me a drink I should be polite and introduce myself.

"Thanks for the drink. I'm Gabriel."

"Lucifer, but you can call me Luc."

"Seriously? Like the Devil?"

"Well, I prefer Morningstar, but yes."

Hot and crazy, just my luck.

"And I'm the Archangel," taunted Gabriel.

"No, you're far better looking than that stuck-up prig."

"Funny guy."

"I haven't been called that for a while," remarked Lucifer with a sly smile. "How do you like the bar?"

"Yeah, it's cool. Interesting décor."

"Glad you appreciate it. I really tried to capture that decadent essence."

Hold on. Does that mean?

"This is *your* bar?" asked Gabriel, slightly impressed.

"Of course. The name didn't give it away?"

He's really committed to his character; I'll give him that. At least he seems harmless…and hot.

"How silly of me."

As they continued to chat pleasantly, their legs rubbed against one another under the bar. There was something about the beautiful bar owner that was very enticing. His convivial manner put Gabriel at ease and all of his worries felt so very far away. He was so caught up in their conversation that it took Trisha a while to get his attention.

"Trevor is taking me back to his place to his see his... wardrobe," stated Trisha with a devious smile. "Will you be alright here?"

"I think I'll be just fine," replied Gabriel, nodding his head towards Lucifer.

"See you tomorrow!"

Lucky girl. Maybe, I'll get lucky too.

A short time later, Gabriel's unspoken wish was granted.

"Would you like to come upstairs to my place?" offered Lucifer, with a distinct twinkle in his eyes. "It's more *private*."

The intonation left little doubt as to what he intended and Gabriel wasn't particularly inclined to object. It had been a while since such an alluring man had paid him so much attention.

"Sure, why not."

At least this day hasn't been all bad.

Following closely behind Lucifer, Gabriel soon found himself getting into an elevator next to the bar's entrance. When the doors closed behind them, Lucifer moved forward and brushed his lips lightly against Gabriel's. Their closeness meant that Lucifer's heady scent of burnt amber wafted into Gabriel's nostrils.

Mmm...so good. I wonder what cologne he wears. It smells divine.

The doors opened into a small foyer with a large crimson metal door. Walking though the doorway, Gabriel saw that the penthouse was like a large cube with glass walls that looked out over the city. The furnishings looked sleek and clean – and expensive.

"This is amazing. You must be loaded!" Immediately regretting his tacky outburst, Gabriel cringed. "Oh, I'm so sorry. I must sound like a country hick."

"Not at all, dear boy. I dabble in all manner of things and it lets me enjoy the finer things in life."

He gave Gabriel a long, lingering kiss then moved off towards the bar that was over by the far-right corner. He soon came back with a cocktail in each hand. Taking a sip, Gabriel discovered that it was even stronger than the ones from the bar below.

They sat on the tawny-colored Chesterfield sofa, looking out over the twinkling lights of the city. Before too long the only gazing they were doing was into each other's eyes a prequel to furiously making out. Admittedly, his head was a little cloudy but Gabriel very much enjoyed what he and Lucifer were doing.

Unsurprisingly, they soon cast off their clothing, helping one another with urgency, until they were stripped down to their underwear. Gabriel felt Lucifer teasing his nipples, rolling the nubs between his thumb and forefinger drawing them into hard, erect, buds. Despite the delightful distraction, Gabriel noted that Lucifer's boxers were silk and felt very expensive and he momentarily felt embarrassed by his own non-brand name cheap plain white jocks. Lucifer soon made it clear, however, that he was far more interested in their contents than their provenance.

Standing up, Lucifer then pulled Gabriel up to face him.

"I think we should move this somewhere more comfortable."

Taking his hand, Lucifer led Gabriel to a huge bed that took up the far-left corner of the penthouse. Lucifer dropped his boxers to reveal nine inches of solid manhood that made Gabriel's mouth water and his heart beat faster. Lucifer then pushed down Gabriel's underwear and the pair tumbled to the bed kissing. Maneuvering around into a sixty-nine, Lucifer easily sucked down Gabriel to the base, while Gabriel did his very best to reciprocate. It was clear to Gabriel that Lucifer was much more experienced in the art of male pleasure than he was, especially when he felt his foreskin being nibbled and teased, while his balls were tugged in an expert manner.

After several pleasurable minutes, Lucifer spun around and moved his face down, licking underneath the low-hanging balls and making his way to Gabriel's rosebud. Tensing up, Gabriel was more than a little apprehensive. He'd never been rimmed before, but soon relaxed into it as the tongue made its way inside. The swirling motion interspersed with quick little jabs felt absolutely incredible, and Gabriel began to moan loudly and writhe upon the bed. As Lucifer continued to eat with gusto, it seemed as if the tongue was going impossibly far inside.

Gabriel was enjoying the rimjob so much that it took him a few moments to realize that a finger had started to work its way in as well. The awareness of the new intruder caused Gabriel to seize up and pull free of Lucifer's enticing embrace.

"I'm sorry," apologized Gabriel, feeling embarrassed by his reaction. "It..."

"Did I hurt you?" asked Lucifer, a look of concern furrowing his brow.

"No, it felt amazing. It's just that…I'm…I'm a…"

"Virgin, I know," replied Lucifer, matter-of-factly.

"But, how? Is it that obvious?"

God, I must be really bad at sex.

"No, I've always been able to tell people's secrets. It's a gift. Don't worry, I have no intention of doing anything to you that you don't agree to."

"That's kind of you. Others haven't been so… understanding."

His strict religious instruction had imprinted on Gabriel the idea of resting unsullied for marriage – even if that might end up being to a guy. That's not to say he was a complete novice, as he'd played around a little bit with the occasional handjob and fellatio, but had never gone all the way. There'd been a few close calls but he'd chickened out at the last moment – much to his partners' collective chagrin.

"I was saving myself. I know it's a stupid idea but it's how I was raised and…I…I just wanted my first time to be special."

Gently taking Gabriel's face in his hands, Lucifer gave him a soft kiss.

"My dear boy, you have nothing to be ashamed of, or to apologize for. Would I be disappointed if we don't go further? Yes, of course. I believe you can see how much I want you. That being said, I much prefer to have a completely willing partner. I assure you, we don't have to do anything you're not ready for. However, if you do decide that you want this, I promise it will be *memorable*."

Lucifer's reassurances and kind manner only increased the desire Gabriel was feeling.

"I'm ready," stated Gabriel, his voice wavering slightly.

"You're sure?"

Am I ready? What about the Reverend's warnings? Should I wait for the one? Maybe Luc is the right guy? There's just something about him that I trust. He seems so…sincere. And he feels fucking amazing.

"Yes." His tone became firmer and determined. "I want this. I want you to be my first."

"As you wish, my dear."

They began kissing again and Gabriel felt his apprehension fading as the pure carnality took over. Lucifer turned Gabriel facedown and kissed along Gabriel's back until he reached the twin mounds and then resumed his rimming. Gabriel had never felt such pleasure and longing. He wanted to be taken, his ass rising instinctively to meet Lucifer's experienced mouth.

"Please fuck me, Luc," moaned Gabriel.

"Only if you're sure."

"Yes, I need it."

"My pleasure, then."

Moving to the side of the bed, Lucifer retrieved protection from the nightstand and was soon suited up in an opaque black condom and began to lubricate Gabriel's virgin passage. He spun Gabriel onto his back, legs spread wide, and took his time introducing his fingers again, stretching and relaxing the hole.

The digits masterfully massaged Gabriel's prostate sending small electric shocks of joy throughout his body. After a few minutes, Gabriel thought he would go mad with desire if Lucifer didn't fuck him right then and there.

Mercifully, Lucifer then positioned himself so that his cockhead kissed the rosebud, teasing the entrance, widening it in slow deliberate circles. As the mushroom-shaped head breached the puckered hole, Gabriel felt a sharp pain but Lucifer's gentle kisses helped him to relax and eased the discomfort. With ever-so-tender thrusting motions, Lucifer worked his cock into the snug passageway, slowly edging his inches inside.

The deeper the manhood pushed inwards, the more the pain turned to pleasure and Gabriel intuitively arched his back and pressed back, encouraging Lucifer to penetrate further. Looking deep into Lucifer's eyes, Gabriel was intoxicated by the need he saw reflected back at him. Gabriel gasped and moaned, feeling wonderfully full and stretched but couldn't believe it as inch after inch kept going inside.

There's no way I can take it all! I can't believe I'm losing my virginity to a stranger, but it feels so right! Like it was meant to be. Why did I wait so long?

Eventually, Gabriel felt Lucifer's hips pressed firmly against him and realized with a start that he had Lucifer inside him to the hilt. Bending forward, Lucifer gave Gabriel a series of long languid kisses, as he let the former virgin adjust to the manhood inside of him.

After a few minutes, Lucifer began to make love to Gabriel with slow, steady strokes. Gabriel gripped Lucifer's back, his nails leaving little red indentations, as he was penetrated again and again. His own cock was rock hard and leaking a constant stream of precum all over his firm stomach.

I never want this to end!

An eternity later, Lucifer rolled Gabriel on his side whilst keeping himself fully inside the moist passage. The spinning of the member inside him caused Gabriel to whimper as his insides were stretched as never before. In the new position, Lucifer picked up the pace, much to Gabriel's great delight.

With the faster tempo both men began to gleam with perspiration. The increase in body heat also seemed to intensify Lucifer's heady, smoky amber scent and sent Gabriel's senses into overdrive. The pounding came in bursts, each time driving Gabriel to the very edge and then backing off before he could call out to stop. This went on for hours, as Gabriel bucked and moaned, completely lost in ecstasy.

Eventually taking pity on the poor lad, Lucifer flipped Gabriel around onto his back once more. Grabbing a hold of Gabriel's precum-lacquered cock, Lucifer began to jack it as he renewed his assault on the well-used ass.

Within a minute, Gabriel was quivering as the tingling in his balls grew in strength and his breathing became hitched. All the stimulation had the desired effect and Gabriel cried out as his body shuddered. His balls drew up and his manhood throbbed as it began to shoot ropes of creamy seed that arced into the air and splattered back down upon his glistening chest.

When Gabriel was fully spent, Lucifer leaned forward to give him the gentlest of kisses before slowly pulling out and moving down on the bed beside him. They lay together sweaty and content, and Gabriel felt a broad smile stretching his lips.

That was so worth going to Hades for!

Kissing and caressing each other, the pair stayed locked in an ardent embrace and Gabriel had never been happier. The affection coupled with the pleasing hardness of Lucifer's body against his meant that Gabriel was soon standing to attention once more.

"Now, let's see what you do with this thing," remarked Lucifer, gripping Gabriel's re-aroused manhood.

The suggestion surprised Gabriel. In his limited experience, the guys had only showed interest in deflowering him rather than offering themselves up for his pleasure.

"You mean you want me to…"

"Of course. That's half the fun of playing with men…unless you don't want to?"

This just keeps getting better and better!

"I'd love to!" affirmed Gabriel, as he eagerly jumped from the bed and rolled on a condom.

Once ready, Gabriel positioned himself between his host's outstretched legs and with the guidance of Lucifer's hand he slid just inside the welcoming passage. Fiery warmth engulfed his member and if he hadn't so recently ejaculated he would have undoubtedly cum straight away. His thrusts were tentative at first, but the look of enjoyment on Lucifer's face soon gave him more confidence. As his movements became stronger and deeper, Gabriel felt a primal part of himself come to the fore, nothing else mattering besides the coupling. Filled with strength he didn't know he had, Gabriel spun Lucifer onto his hands and knees and began to hammer away like a man possessed. He repeatedly slapped the side of Lucifer's ass as he fucked him, causing bright red finger marks to appear. Driven by an all-consuming desire, and with one hand gripping Lucifer's hip, Gabriel reached forward and grabbed Lucifer by the hair and pulled back. A loud grunt of appreciation only encouraged Gabriel in his forceful treatment. Pulling out roughly, he flipped Lucifer back around and plunged his manhood back inside the willing hole.

In the home stretch, Gabriel was battering away with all his might, his breath ragged as sweat dripped off of his thrusting body. Looking down, Gabriel could see Lucifer's handsome features contorted in a mixture of surprise and pure joy. Moments later, Lucifer's cockhead erupted, sending thick spurts of semen flying into the air, the first hitting Gabriel on the chin, while the rest decorated Lucifer's well-built torso. The erotic sight was more than enough to push Gabriel over the edge and he yelled in pleasure, as his load burst from his cock and filled his protective sheath. He collapsed down onto Lucifer, the sweat and seed forming a sticky layer between their spent bodies.

They stayed like this for a few minutes, holding one another tightly, neither saying a word as their breathing returned to normal.

I can die happy!

"That's some God-given talent, Mister," declared Lucifer. "Not what I expected from a virgin, but you took it like a man and gave it back threefold. I haven't been ridden like that since the French Revolution... those were the days. Mark my words, my dear, you were born for this."

"Thanks." Gabriel had never felt so unbelievably satisfied. "I don't know what came over me. It was like you released something inside of me. And it is my name I guess."

"Sorry?"

"My last name is Dieudonné. It means..."

"Gift of God, yes I know." An odd thoughtful expression settled upon Lucifer's face. "I wonder..."

"Yes?"

"Oh, I...I was just thinking of an old story. Nothing to worry your pretty head about."

They lay there together in the afterglow, their fingers linked as they cuddled. It was only the first of many bouts that evening, the duo taking turns to defile one another. Eventually, exhaustion claimed Gabriel and just as the sun's first rays started to pour slowly into the apartment, he fell into a contented slumber, wrapped up securely in Lucifer's magnificently, strong arms.

* * *

Waking up midway through the following afternoon, Gabriel was still floating on cloud nine. He felt a bit sore and well used but it had definitely been worth it.

"Good afternoon, sleepyhead," greeted Lucifer, as he entered the room with a tray bearing pastries and coffee. "I thought you might sleep the entire day away."

Overcome with emotion of the enormity of what had happened from the night before, Gabriel temporarily lost control of his mouth.

"I think I love you, Luc," gushed Gabriel.

"Ah, sweet boy. A good cocking will do that to you."

"I'm sorry, I don't know why I just blurted that out."

"You don't love me...but *lust me*, most definitely. And the feeling is utterly reciprocated. It wasn't so horrible to sacrifice your virginity to me, was it?" drawled Lucifer, emanating a grand air of mischief.

"Hell, no."

"And believe me, I'm honored to have been your first...and second and third..."

"The pleasure was mine," grinned Gabriel.

Placing the tray in the middle of the bed, Lucifer climbed in beside Gabriel and they began to eat. Lost in memories from the night before, Gabriel was a little startled when Lucifer asked an unexpected question.

"What is it you truly desire?" inquired Lucifer, his eyes glinting with curiosity.

"Besides you?" joked Gabriel, although there was a kernel of truth to his words.

"Yes, what do you want most in your life."

"The same as every actor in this city – fame and fortune! But seriously, I just want to be able to make a decent living from being on stage. It's been a dream of mine since I was a little boy. I'd love to have audiences applauding me…maybe win an award…or a dozen. Make the switch to Hollywood, become an A-lister and then I'll never have to go back and live that small-town existence and deal with that sanctimonious reverend and his horrible bigoted views. Sorry, for rambling, I really don't know why I told you all that."

Why am I such a babbling idiot? Is it the sex? He is so easy to talk to.

"People usually confide in me, it's part of my charm." Lucifer gave Gabriel a disarming smile. "What would you say if I told you that I could help get your stunning career on the stage and all the rest you covet?"

"How? Are you in the industry? Oh God, that sounds so desperate. I'm so rude, I don't think I've even asked what you do besides owning the bar."

"We were a little, ah, *distracted*. Besides, I told you who I am."

"Yes, yes, you're Lucifer," teased Gabriel "The Devil, I remember."

"Exactly, dear boy."

"Prove it," scoffed Gabriel. "Show me your horns."

"Alright then."

All of a sudden, Lucifer's eyes changed from their bewitching emerald shade to a glowing blood-red and two curved, midnight-black horns sprouted from the top of his head. Gabriel felt his mouth drop open but not a sound came out. No matter how hard his instincts were yelling at him to flee as fast as possible, he felt glued to the spot. It was then that he started hyperventilating and began to sweat profusely.

"Come now," placated Lucifer, his eyes resuming their previous color and his horns retracting. "No need to get all worked up."

"But, but, but…"

"I know it can be all very frightening to start with but once you get to know me I'm not so bad…mostly."

Leaning forward, Lucifer ran his hands up and down Gabriel's arms, which had a calming, almost mesmerizing, effect. Gabriel felt his breathing and his heartbeat slow down to almost normal levels and the urge to vomit passed.

"Better?" asked Lucifer.

Gabriel nodded dumbly in response, still not quite able to process what had just happened.

This can't be real. Am I dreaming? Did I lose my virginity to the goddamn Devil?

"I can make all your dreams come true," continued Lucifer in his silky-smooth baritone. "How do you think half the celebrities get to where they are? I mean, does anyone honestly believe that the world would be so obsessed with the Kardashians if there hadn't been some sort of otherworldly manipulation?"

"That actually makes a lot of sense." A sudden thought gripped Gabriel. "Do you only seek out virgins?"

"Dear me, no. I much prefer *experienced* partners. Although, I'm starting to think that we were destined to meet." His brow furrowed slightly before his face took on its habitual nonchalant regard. "Anyway, what do you say? Your soul for your wildest dreams?"

"I...I don't...I..."

"I'm a patient man. How about I give you a day to decide. If you want to take the deal meet me back here at six o'clock tomorrow evening. If the answer, is 'no' then don't come and I promise you'll never see me again."

Gabriel's body cried out at the idea of never again experiencing the pleasure of Lucifer's touch.

"Never?"

"As much as a sacrifice it would be to leave you unmolested, I promise to let you live the rest of your life as you chose."

"I have a day to decide?" confirmed Gabriel, already starting to debate the offer.

"That's right. Now, let's finish up breakfast, then my driver will see you home so you can rest up and sleep on your decision. I'd love to keep you here all day, but quite frankly if you stay I'll just keep playing with you until you're all worn out."

In spite of his predicament, Gabriel found that he was ravenously hungry and eagerly finished off the remaining pastries, before bidding Lucifer a hasty goodbye. On the way back to his apartment, in the backseat of Lucifer's limo, Gabriel's mind was spinning.

What the fuck have I got myself into? It would be nice to be driven around in limos all the time though. Is it worth my soul? Am I seriously considering this? I mean the sex was awesome, but still. What on earth am I going to do?

* * *

Gabriel spent the rest of the day, and a great deal of the night, debating with himself about the merits and drawbacks of the deal. He toyed with talking to Trisha about it, but feared that she wouldn't believe him.

I wouldn't believe me either.

Fortunately, she was so engrossed by relaying her adventures with the barman from the previous evening that she barely noticed Gabriel's own distracted mood. Later that evening, Trisha disappeared off to Trevor's apartment – evidently keen for round two – leaving Gabriel to toss and turn in his bed, feeling conflicted and a little excited.

Finally, he fell into a dreamless sleep just before the dawn. Opportunely, he didn't have work the next day and was free to spend it obsessively going over his rather unexpected encounter. Naturally, this is exactly what he did.

Can I really give up my soul? What's it ever done for me? Won't a life of fame and fortune be worth it? Maybe Hell won't be so bad.

One hour before he was due to return to Lucifer's apartment, Gabriel knew what he had to do. He grabbed his satchel and raced downstairs to jump on the subway. At the appointed time, Gabriel stood outside the large red door and rang the doorbell.

His usual butterflies of nervousness felt like they were dancing with elephants in his stomach. A few seconds passed, giving Gabriel second thoughts. He had begun to turn around when the door suddenly opened and revealed Lucifer standing there in a black silk robe. Gabriel's eyes immediately travelled downwards, as the robe was hanging open and Lucifer wasn't wearing a stitch of clothing underneath. Everything was as magnificent as he remembered and Gabriel had to force himself to close his mouth and return his gaze to the Devil's handsome face.

"Why, hello there," smiled Lucifer, obviously well aware of the effect he was having on Gabriel. "I was hoping you'd show up."

"I've thought about it and I've decided that…"

Lucifer silenced him with a kiss that led from the front door to the bedroom, leaving a trail of wildly flung clothes in their wake.

"Pleasure before business, Gabe," purred Lucifer, when they broke for air.

Before he knew it, Lucifer had Gabriel flat on his back with his legs spread wide. Moments later, Gabriel felt the sensation of all those thick, lovely inches sliding inside of him and sending him to seventh heaven. It felt even longer than before, reaching even further inside, touching previously unexplored depths.

"It's bigger!" gasped Gabriel.

"Why, yes it is," agreed Lucifer, withdrawing himself to reveal the now thirteen solid inches of manhood. "This is my true length, but I didn't want to brutalize your poor ass too badly on your first time."

"That was considerate of you."

"I thought so." Lucifer winked, as he retook Gabriel.

An hour or so later when they'd unloaded a few times apiece; it was time to get down to business.

"What will it be?" asked Lucifer, lightly stroking Gabriel's chest. "Will you give yourself to me?"

Last chance to get out of this whole thing. Get up and go! What the fuck am I doing?

"Yes," stated Gabriel, a slight tremble to his voice. "I will sign over my soul."

"Wonderful." Lucifer clicked his fingers and a large parchment appeared on the bed next to them. "Read it over, carefully. There's no changing your mind once you've signed."

Standing up, Gabriel took the parchment in hand began to go over it with more attention than he'd ever read anything. For the most part, it was as Lucifer promised; in exchange for relinquishing his soul he would have his dream of stardom. There was, however, a slight catch that Gabriel hadn't been prepared for.

"Hold on! This says that my soul is collectible in thirty years on October 31st? I thought I'd have until…well, until I died."

"You do, dear boy."

"What?" cried Gabriel, leaping up from the bed. "How can you know that?"

"Oh, didn't I mention that part?" remarked Lucifer with a rueful smile. "As ruler of the underworld I have knowledge over all matters death-related, my brother Azraël keeps me up-to-date. And that includes when your time is up."

"I'm going to die in *thirty* years? I won't have had enough time to have a mid-life crisis by then!"

Rising from the bed, Lucifer moved towards Gabriel and drew him into a tender embrace. Gabriel resisted at first, but his body betrayed him with its instinctual response to Lucifer's touch.

"Look, you can sign and you get to live your dream life or not sign and live an ordinary life but either way you'll still be dead on that date. Isn't it better to have the life you want instead of always wondering what could have been?"

I don't want to be ordinary.

"I guess," admitted Gabriel. "OK, I'll sign. Do I have to sign it in blood?"

"Any bodily fluid will do."

Turning so that he was standing behind Gabriel facing the bed, Lucifer grabbed a hold of Gabriel's cock and massaged it. As expected, this caused Gabriel to writhe in pleasure and within seconds the member became engorged and then spurted a large, load of white seed all over the parchment.

"There, all signed."

What did I just do?

"Does that mean that there will there be a hoard of paparazzi waiting outside for me?" inquired Gabriel, only half-joking.

"Not just yet, but don't worry you'll get exactly what you asked for. Now that the business side is completed, how about a bit more pleasure?"

Without waiting for an answer, Lucifer spun Gabriel around took his mouth into a savage kiss. Unsurprisingly, Lucifer was already hard and ready to go and Gabriel wasn't feeling inclined to resist – his body innately aroused by Lucifer's. Their play went on for hours with Gabriel losing track of just how many times he'd been penetrated, although he did his fair share of forceful plowing in return. The exertion took its toll and Gabriel closed his eyes, intending on resting only for a few minutes, his body agreeably intertwined with Lucifer's.

When he awoke, Gabriel found himself tucked up in his own bed with only the phantom cock sensation in his ass stopping him from simply believing it was all a dream.

How did I get here? Have I done the right thing? When am I going to be famous already?

* * *

Almost a month passed with no miraculous changes in his life and Gabriel was beginning to grow concerned. He'd had five auditions over the past few weeks but hadn't heard back about any of them, which was discouraging to say the least. After another week went by, Gabriel returned to Lucifer's apartment but when he knocked there was no answer and no signs of life. He didn't even have a phone number to call. Disheartened, Gabriel was starting to think he must have had some sort of mental breakdown. If that wasn't bad enough, Gabriel found that he didn't feel whole since the last time he'd seen Lucifer. Not only did he miss the incredible sex, the surge of emotion he'd felt for Lucifer after their first night together hadn't really dissipated.

You can't be in love with the Devil. If he even is the Devil. Did I make it all up? Guess I get to keep my soul then. I suppose I should go home and get ready for work.

As he was climbing back onto the subway, his phone began to vibrate in his pocket. By the display, Gabriel saw that it was Shelley calling.

Probably another rejection.

"Listen Doll, I've got another audition for you tomorrow afternoon. Can you make it?"

"I'm supposed to be working but I should be able to swap out with someone."

Not sure there's much point, though.

"It's actually for one of my other clients, who has a show that's opening in a month. He's an up-and-coming playwright, Charlie Redman. The guy they'd had lined up broke his arm in a motorbike accident and they're desperate. The play is going to be in an off-off-Broadway venue. It's a comedy and there's some singing and dancing. The pay's not great but you never know where it might lead."

"I guess there's no harm in trying."

"Thatta boy! I'll email you the details."

What have I got to lose…apart from my pride and dignity?

The following afternoon, Gabriel arrived promptly at the allocated time and was shown into the small, dingy theatre.

"Hi, you must be Gabriel," greeted a handsome man with auburn hair and freckles. "I'm Charlie. It's a very small production and I'll be handling the auditions and directing."

"Thanks so much for giving me this opportunity."

"Shelley tells me that you're amazing and she says the same about me so it must be true," laughed Charlie. "How about you take these pages and hop up on the stage."

I wouldn't mind sleeping with him for the part. Damn what did Lucifer do to me?

As it turned out there was no need for any casting couch shenanigans as Charlie offered him the job as soon as he finished the audition.

"Fantastic! Shelley was right. I think we've found our new leading man."

"Really?" burbled Gabriel, as he tried not to cry with happiness. "Oh my god, thank you so much!"

"Now, because it's such a tight timeframe we're going to be rehearsing pretty much every day and most nights. Are you able to commit to that?"

I'll have to quit my job, there's no way I can do both. I have enough saved to get by for about a month and a half before I starve to death. I guess I must take a leap of faith.

"Yes, yes, I can."

A whirlwind of rehearsals soon followed and Gabriel found his nervousness increasing as opening night approached with an alarming speed. He worried about his performance, worried about his lack of employment if things didn't work out and most of all he was terrified that no one would even show up.

"I'll bring everyone from work," assured Trisha. "They'll see how brilliant you are and it will be a smashing success. My best friend's going to be famous!"

"From your lips to God's ears."

Or Lucifer's.

True to her word, Trisha arrived at the opening performance with twenty people in tow. Unfortunately, there weren't too many others but Gabriel still managed to keep positive.

I need to do damn best no matter the size of the audience. This is what I wanted. Don't blow it.

Miraculously, the performance went off without a hitch. The audience loved it, especially Trisha's fashion friends, giving the cast a rousing round of applause. Rave reviews and word of mouth soon had the reservation line ringing hot and by the end of their initial run they were playing to packed houses. Indeed, they were so successful that the production moved to a bigger theatre for a month-long season. By the time the production closed, Gabriel had two more acting jobs lined up. It seemed like his luck was finally turning around.

Thank you, Luc.

* * *

Twenty-nine years after he had signed the fateful parchment, Gabriel was lying facedown, naked on a massage table. A large, soft, navy-blue towel covered his midsection and he was patiently awaiting the arrival of Sven – six feet of pure, muscled manhood with magic hands that could ferret out the most stubborn of knots. The strapping Swede had been helping relieve Gabriel's tension once a week for the past few years, and always with a discreet happy ending.

The last three decades had been good to Gabriel and despite his fifty-three years of age he barely looked a day over forty – due in no small part to the expert work of his trusted plastic surgeon. His career had gone from strength to strength, with a successful transition from Broadway to Hollywood and a string of awards that made him one of the most bankable stars of the day.

After the first decade, Gabriel had stopped dwelling on the deal. For his own ego, he chose to believe that his great success was due to his talent and luck rather than a Faustian bargain. Eventually, he convinced himself that it had all been his overactive imagination brought on by mind-blowing sex with a gorgeous, albeit delusional, man. Otherwise, he'd have to admit that his days were numbered and an eternity in Hell awaited him.

Making a deal with the Devil. Ridiculous. Honestly, what was I thinking? Absolute nonsense.

He'd been lying there for slightly longer than usual and was starting to become restless when he heard the door open and solid footsteps enter into the room.

"You got your work cut out for you today, Sven. I locked up my back in…"

"I'm sorry, but Sven couldn't make it today," said a deep and distantly familiar voice. "But I'm sure that you'll find me a more than adequate replacement."

Gabriel then felt his towel being pushed up before two strong hands spread his ass cheeks apart and a long tongue pierced his rosebud. He gasped in pleasure and was lost in the pure bliss of it for a few seconds before his brain finally switched into gear and he realized who was in the room with him.

Jumping up from the massage table, Gabriel whirled around to face his old acquaintance, who appeared untouched by the ravages of time and was practically busting out of a crisp white spa uniform. The sight of Lucifer instantly reignited a flame of emotion that Gabriel had been doing his very best to keep well snuffed out. Terrified as he was, there was still a very large part of Gabriel that was happy to see Lucifer – and not just his nether regions.

"Luc? No, it can't be. I imagined all that. What did you to do Sven?"

"Is that any way to greet an old friend?" grinned Lucifer. "No need to worry about Sven, he's sleeping off the best fuck of his life. I can certainly see why you have a weekly appointment with him."

Remembering well Lucifer's talent for carnality, Gabriel felt a pang of envy towards his masseur. Indeed, his devilish encounter all those years ago had given Gabriel quite the appetite for male flesh, always chasing the high he'd felt with Lucifer. Undeniably, he'd had some ridiculously hot times in the intervening years, but no one else ever managed to quite send him to those rapturous heights.

Gracefully leaping over the massage table, Lucifer then pinned Gabriel firmly against the wall. Despite his fear, his manhood was at full mast and Gabriel could feel a reciprocal hardening in Lucifer's crotch pressing into him. No man had ever penetrated him so deeply, both physically and emotionally. His body was yearning for Lucifer to take him as he had before.

Goddamn I need him. Stop thinking with your cock. He wants to take my soul and I've only got a year to go.

"You've certainly done well for yourself, since last we met, I must say. Three Tony awards, two Emmys and an Oscar! Not bad at all for a small-town boy."

Trying to keep his voice steady and ignore his raging erection, Gabriel went on the offensive.

"What are you doing here?" demanded Gabriel angrily. "It isn't time yet."

"Why, this is your friendly one-year reminder, of course," stated Lucifer with a wicked grin. "And I must say, compliments to your surgeons, you look thoroughly delicious."

Regardless of the dire situation, Gabriel couldn't help but be flattered.

"You really think so? I thought the last nip and tuck might have been a tad too tight."

"Nonsense, my dear. Although that will hardly be a concern for you too much longer…unless."

Grasping desperately for any escape to his predicament, Gabriel's pulse began to race even faster as a sliver of optimism flitted into his heart.

"Unless what?"

"Well…I don't usually do this for my *contractees*, but you were such a delectable treat when we first met and I must admit you do intrigue me. You're not quite what I expected, at all," mused Lucifer. "As I was saying, there may be a loophole of sorts."

"Loophole? Tell me! I'll do anything. Just tell m…"

Lucifer hushed him with a forceful kiss, which went on for some minutes. Gabriel began to melt into Lucifer's arms before he once more came to his senses and broke from the embrace.

"Tell me, please," he begged.

"I could void your contract if you are able to find me another soul to make a deal in your place. They'll have the same opportunity you had, to achieve their fondest desires, with my getting their soul afterwards."

Could I sacrifice someone else?

"Does that mean that I won't die in a year then?" queried Gabriel, the desperation clear in his voice.

"Oh no, dear boy. I'm afraid that is inevitable. It will just mean that when your time comes, you'll be free to go... *upstairs*."

Disdain dripped from Lucifer's last word and he grimaced.

"I guess that's better."

"Not if you ask me, but to each his own," sighed Lucifer, with a touch of aloofness. "Alright, now that's sorted, how about I give you that happy ending."

Powerless to resist, Gabriel allowed himself to fall back into Lucifer's embrace, with both the towel and the white uniform hastily flung to the floor. Moments later, they began to mate with raw animal lust, as Lucifer penetrated Gabriel and rode him hard against the wall.

Damn, I've missed this. Thank goodness the walls are thick.

The stimulation was all too overpowering for Gabriel and the load that had been building in his balls soon found itself sprayed over the sea-green wall in front of him. This was followed in short order by the hot seed of Lucifer coating his insides, which tingled in an agreeable fashion. Once done, Lucifer gave Gabriel a peck on the lips.

"Here, you can hold onto this," he said throwing him the dreaded parchment. "It's indestructible by mortal hands so I have no fear of your trying to destroy it. Call my name when you're ready to deal, my dear."

He disappeared in a red flash of light, leaving the scent of burnt amber lingering in the room. Sinking to the floor, Gabriel's mind raced with the possibilities afforded by this new information.

Who do I know that deserves to go to Hell?

* * *

Over the following months, Gabriel turned the issue over and over in his mind, deciding upon and then discarding choice after choice. Frankly, there'd been no shortage of people that he'd told to go to Hell already but he was having trouble settling on someone who truly merited it. There was also the problem of believability.

Who will believe me? I'll probably end up in a nuthouse if I start going around telling people I've made a deal with the Devil and they can too.

At the eleven-month mark Gabriel was becoming desperate and he finally picked the one person that he'd actually thought of first, namely his ex-wife, Diana Jackson. These days the pair only spoke sporadically and had a love-hate relationship that had long exhausted its quota of love. In all honesty, they'd only married at the behest of their agents. At the time they were both up for major roles in the same blockbuster action film and their reputations were in need of a boost – their shared passion for partying and affairs with thoroughly unsuitable partners wasn't doing them any favors. The publicity generated by the spontaneous nuptials proved to be the winning factor and they both snagged the roles in what turned out to be the biggest earning film of the year. While 'Maximum Deceit' was a box office success, the same could not be said for their marriage, which scarcely lasted till the film was out of the cinemas. They fought constantly and while the sex had been decent, they weren't compatible in any other respect. It was the last time that Gabriel had bothered with matrimony...with either sex.

Regardless, it had been extremely beneficial for their careers, with both enjoying great success over the following decades, although lately that hadn't been the case for Diana. Gabriel couldn't remember the last time his ex-wife had a hit and at her age the roles were becoming increasingly scarce on the ground. It was a nasty double standard that men were allowed to get older on screen but women were most certainly not.

I'd be doing her a favor. By sending her to Hell? She could probably teach them a thing or two about torture, though.

Forced into action by his looming deadline, Gabriel called Diana and asked to meet for lunch at his apartment that weekend – to which she hesitantly agreed.

An hour after the arranged lunchtime, Diana arrived looking well put together as always, in a smart white pantsuit that showed off her lithe figure and complimented both her emerald eyes and her raven locks that were arranged upon her head in a becoming fashion. In her mid-fifties, her face was conspicuously line-free.

She's still beautiful...on the outside.

"Darling, sorry I'm late, but the traffic was horrendous," sighed Diana. "Forgive me?"

Yeah right, she's never been on time in her life.

"Of course," replied Gabriel cordially, not wanting to start one of their habitual fights. "Please come in."

They sat down to a delicious Cesar salad, followed by pesto chicken pasta that Gabriel had ordered in from a nearby Italian restaurant – he'd never been one for cooking. After thirty minutes or so of small talk, Diana came to the point.

"Why did you really invite me to lunch, Gabe?"

"What if I could offer you a way to get back on top?"

"Of you? I don't think so, darling."

"Don't be preposterous. I meant your career."

"I'm doing fine."

"Really? When was the last time you were in front of a camera? And I don't mean that ridiculous slasher flick you did last year."

He saw the look of hurt in her eyes and immediately regretted his cruelty.

"I'm sorry, that was uncalled for. You're a brilliant actress and I think you deserve more. Please let me explain."

"Go on," said Diana frostily.

"It's about how I became so successful."

"On your back?" taunted Diana, more than a trace of malice in her voice.

"OK, I deserved that. But you're right...in a way. Many years ago, when I was just starting out I made a deal that ensured my career and I can offer it to you too."

"I'm listening."

Here goes nothing.

"I signed a contract with the Devil. My soul in exchange for my fantasy life."

"You're pathetic!" spat Diana. "What the fuck are you talking about? Is this some kind of joke? Just like our marriage."

"Oh, please, I think we both made a wreck of that relationship." Remembering the reason for the lunch, Gabriel stopped himself before launching into a tirade. "I know it sounds outrageous but it's true. Don't you deserve a second chance?"

"Of course I do, but that doesn't mean I have to listen to your crazed delusions. Even if I were to believe this nonsense, then why would you offer it to me?"

"Because you have to sign over your soul and I thought you'd have no problem with it."

The words were out of his mouth before he could stop them and he knew that it was the exact wrong thing to say. It hadn't been the first time he'd accused her of being soulless.

Why does she always have this effect on me?

"Charming," sneered Diana. "I'm leaving."

"Wait, I can prove it. I can show you my contract."

"Well, this oughta be good," remarked Diana, sarcasm heavy in her tone.

Hastily, Gabriel went to the large redwood bureau in his study and retrieved the parchment from the locked bottom drawer.

"See, it's real," insisted Gabriel, brandishing the contract.

"What are those stains on it? Are you showing me some trumped up devil agreement with fucking cum stains on it?"

Damn, I forgot about that.

"I…ahh…it's how he wanted me to sign."

"I don't know what drugs you're on but you need help, you loon. I'm not listening to you another moment."

"No wait. Lucifer, I demand you show yourself."

39

Despite her earlier skepticism, Diana looked around the room cautiously for a second and when nothing happened she smirked and turned to leave.

"Do me a favor and lose my number, jackass!"

She stormed out and slammed the door behind her, leaving a very irate Gabriel standing holding the parchment.

"Luc, where the fuck are you? Goddamn it!"

Suddenly, there was a small red flash and Lucifer appeared, clad only in a black leather harness and matching black gloves with his erect manhood on full display. Despite his anger, Gabriel couldn't help but to be aroused at the sight.

"Sorry, I was...*occupied*," drawled Lucifer. "Did you need something?"

"I was trying to get someone else to sign but now she thinks I'm nuts," lamented Gabriel. "And it's all your fault!"

"You manage to convince her to come back and I'll be happy to prove her wrong."

"That'll take a miracle."

Just then there his front door was flung open and in walked a still clearly furious Diana.

"I left my damn keys on the..." Catching sight of a glistening Lucifer she stopped midsentence. "What the..."

"Lucifer Morningstar, at your service."

"You can't be...you're really *him*?"

"Yes, my dear."

"How do I know you're not some stripper he's hired to play into his delusion?" mocked Diana.

As he'd done with Gabriel, Lucifer changed his appearance to a far more demonic one, his eyes ablaze and horns upon his head. To her credit, Diana stood there calmly with a look of quiet determination about her. After a few moments she spoke in a cool, level voice.

"Can you really do what he says?"

"I most certainly can, Madam. Your heartfelt desire for the measly price of your eternal soul."

"I need to think about it."

"Certainly. Why don't we meet back here in a week's time, say four o'clock, and then you can give me your answer?"

"A week?" interjected Gabriel. "You only gave me a day!"

"What can I say, I'm getting generous in my old age." Turning back to Diana he continued. "What do you say, my dear? I don't mean to be impatient but I have some *unfinished business* in Sydney."

"I'll be here."

"Good job. See you both then."

And then he disappeared in the same red flash, leaving Gabriel and Diana staring at one another.

"That was…unexpected," commented Diana after a few seconds. "Well then, I'll see you in a week."

She turned and was almost out the door when Gabriel was caught be a sudden bout of conscience.

"Diana."

"Yes?"

"Think about it carefully."

"Oh, I will."

She left in a far less dramatic fashion, closing the door gently. Standing alone in his apartment, Gabriel had the tiniest pricking of his conscience.

I hope I've done the right thing.

* * *

The following Saturday, Gabriel was in a state of extreme agitation. All week long he'd been swinging between the extremes of being overjoyed that he'd found a replacement and then stricken with guilt about the fate to which he was condemning her. There was a tiny voice in the back of his mind that was becoming progressively louder as the weekend drew near.

I should be paying the price myself. Don't condemn her. No matter how much she may deserve it.

Diana was the first to arrive, uncharacteristically early in fact.

"Is he here yet?" she demanded as soon as Gabriel opened the door.

"And hello to you too, Diana, pleasant weather we're having."

"Sorry, Gabe. I'm just keen to get this over with."

"Are you sure you want to do this?" insisted Gabriel, his conscience overcoming him. "It's a big price for your career."

"What's gotten into you? First off, you practically forced this opportunity on me and now you're trying to talk me out of it. Have you been self-medicating again? I thought that last trip to rehab stuck. It doesn't matter; I've made up my mind. I want this!"

A bright red flash interrupted their conversation, as Lucifer materialized – this time wearing a tailored navy suit. Even though he was distracted by his inner turmoil, Gabriel appreciated Lucifer's appearance.

He looks good in anything. I wonder if he'll stay after the signing to have some fun. Focus, Gabriel!

"Diana, Gabriel," greeted Lucifer. "Ready?"

"Yes, I am," declared Diana. "Where do I sign?"

Lucifer clicked his fingers and an identical looking parchment to Gabriel's appeared on the dining table.

"So, I need to do this in…blood?"

"No, a pen will do."

"What? But you made me…" began Gabriel.

"Hush now. You enjoyed it," grinned Lucifer.

Grabbing a pen from her handbag, Diana moved towards the table. She leaned forward and was about to sign when something in Gabriel snapped and he rushed over and snatched the pen from her hand.

"No, don't. You can't sign it. I'm only letting you do this so that I don't have to go to Hell," confessed Gabriel. "It was selfish of me and I'm sorry."

"Well, that doesn't surprise me in the slightest," snarled Diana. "But, I don't care. I'm still going through with it."

"What?!"

"I said, *I don't care.* I want my second chance and I'll do whatever it takes."

"It's not worth it. I can't let you suffer for what I did. No matter the history between us you don't deserve to be damned for my actions. And if I don't agree you can't have your contract."

"Is that true?" asked Diana turning to Lucifer.

"Sorry, my dear, but that was the arrangement."

Whirling around to face Gabriel, Diana's face was full of fury.

"You're pathetic, you know that. I should've known you would ruin this for me just like you've done for everything else. You're so fucking selfish. You deserve to go to straight to Hell."

Snatching her handbag, Diana ran from the house and downstairs to the street. Not watching where she was going, she rushed straight into the path of an oncoming bus. Watching from the window, Gabriel cried out to warn her but she was too far away to hear. Fortunately, the screeching of tires alerted her to her dire predicament and she threw herself out of the way. Picking herself up back of the ground, she turned and shot another filthy look up at Gabriel and stomped off.

Thank the gods! I never wanted her dead.

"Did you do that?" asked Gabriel in an accusatory tone.

"Oh, please that was karma. That woman is a nightmare. Don't worry, she has another good twenty years to go…although I would've had fun torturing her for an eternity."

"Alright, good. The last thing I need is to feel responsible for killing her. I guess we might as well get this over and done with, there's no one to trade with now."

"Not so fast, Mister. I must admit you surprised me. I wasn't sure you would choose to be so selfless, it showed real strength of character, heroic even. Truthfully, I did have an inkling that you wouldn't be able to go through with it."

"This was a test?"

"Of sorts."

"So, I passed? I don't have to go?" asked Gabriel, his voice brimming with optimism.

"Sorry, but a deal's a deal, my dear."

"Oh." His disappointment was painfully obvious. "I guess you're right."

"Chin up, you still have another week to go. I'll be back to get you when it's your time. Live it up…while you can."

And with that he disappeared in a red flash.

I'll never get used to that.

* * *

One week later, at twenty minutes to midnight, Lucifer came for Gabriel. His last week had been fun, mostly fucking and partying, but when it came to the final day the hedonistic desire left him. The sobering thought of what was to come made him settle down at home instead. He even forwent his usual Halloween party, which always ended up in an orgy of eager young men looking for their chance of stardom through whatever pleasurable means necessary.

His death had been far less dramatic than Gabriel had imagined; an aneurism took him in his sleep. Naturally, there was a great outpouring of love on social media, as is often the case when celebrities depart the mortal coil, but he'd soon been replaced in the news cycle by the latest wacky antics of a drugged-up reality TV star and his on again/off again equally disturbed girlfriend.

Climbing out of bed and leaving his body behind Gabriel turned to Lucifer.

"It's all over then?" questioned Gabriel sadly.

"Just the beginning, my dear," replied Lucifer, a roguish spark in his eyes. "You know, you're the first person who has ever come willingly and I have a proposition for you."

"Yes?"

"Marry me."

Has he started the torture already?

"You can't be serious?"

"Oh but I am, my dear. To be honest, I've developed a bit of a soft spot for you...very unusual, as I don't tend to get attached to mortals. When we first met, you reminded me of an ancient prophecy. It said that if I faithfully carried out my duties of meting out punishment and justice throughout the ages, then I would be rewarded by a gift from above; pure of body with the heart and soul of an angel, and who fornicated like a demon. Pretty much describes you to a tee, really. Of course, most of the time those things were made up by drunk old druids and are about as accurate as a newspaper horoscope, but I've felt that you were different from the beginning. You must admit that our couplings are divine and I know that you've been pining for me since our first encounter. Besides I've had enough wives over the centuries but never had a husband. What do you say?"

Could this be my escape? It seems far too good to be true.

"What happened to your previous spouses?" inquired Gabriel, a slight feeling of dread in the pit of his stomach.

"Banishment, imprisonment...the usual."

"I see. And how do I know that wouldn't happen to me?"

"Well, now, that's the adventure isn't it," purred Lucifer playfully.

"So...I still have to go to Hell?"

"Yes, but there are a lot of fringe benefits."

"Such as?"

"Well, not being tortured is a pretty big one. And then there's the eternal youth in the afterlife and getting to fuck around with me every day till the end of time."

What have I go to lose? I died and now I'm getting married? I certainly never thought that's how things would end up.

"Done."

Lucifer took Gabriel by the hand and they disappeared in the blink of an eye. That had been just over a century ago and Gabriel had yet to regret his decision. They'd married that day in a discreet ceremony officiated by the Lucifer's brother, Azraël, the Angel of Death himself – a surprisingly funny guy. Then they honeymooned on a private island for around a decade or so, both of them preferring hotter climes. As promised in death, Lucifer had taken Gabriel back to his more youthful appearance and there had been quite a good deal of delectable fornication over the years.

Unlike other relationships where things had become stale in the boudoir after a while, it wasn't the case for the happy couple. Granted they did pop upstairs to the occasional orgy at the Vatican – they tended to be the best – and gave the odd gorgeous mortal a night they'd never forget.

Behind him, Gabriel heard the clatter of cloven hooves enter the room. Without looking, Gabriel knew that Lucifer was in one his more recognizable forms – menacingly tall, scarlet-skinned with black pointed horns. His ability to take on any appearance was another factor that helped keep their passion alive.

"You know I don't like to wake up alone," pouted Gabriel, in a mock-petulant manner.

"I'm sorry, Gabe, it was a work thing. I had to appear to a bunch of teenagers playing with a Ouija board and scare the bejeezus out of them."

"Sounds more like fun than work to me," huffed Gabriel, without any real conviction.

"Can't it be both?" Lucifer moved in behind him and wrapped his powerful red arms around Gabriel. "Besides, I'm sure I know how to make it up to you, my dear."

"Oh, do you just?" countered Gabriel, who was already tilting his hips back in anticipation of what was to come.

He felt the bulbous head of Lucifer's cock press into his rosebud and begin snaking its way inside of him. The wide thirteen inches, curving in a way no mortal manhood could, penetrating and probing his insides.

"Feel better?" murmured Lucifer, as he nuzzled Gabriel's neck.

"Yes," panted Gabriel, who'd been prompting his husband into this very action.

Gabriel's hands were splayed against the glass, as he braced himself for the inevitable heavy pounding he was due. He spread his legs to allow his husband even greater access. The interaction was heightened by knowing that their encounter was being broadcast live into the cells of the prisoners likely to be the most tormented by the sight of a big red demon sodomizing a human.

Starting with long, slow, powerful thrusts, Lucifer penetrated to his husband's innermost depths and then built up to a good hammering. Lucifer moved his hands to Gabriel's hips to keep them locked in position as he savaged the ass with all his otherworldly might. The fucking would have undoubtedly destroyed a human, tearing him apart from the inside. To Gabriel, however, it felt absolutely heavenly.

All good things must come to an end and the constant overstimulation of his prostate drove Gabriel over the edge. His balls contracted moments before his cock throbbed and spurted uncontrollably, spraying his seed all over the clear glass. Lucifer wasn't far behind and shot deep inside Gabriel, sending a pleasant warming sensation all throughout his body, as it was absorbed into him. Gabriel's body pulsed with the power of it and it brought a smile to his lips.

Lucifer slapped Gabriel on the ass before withdrawing and then gave his husband a warm kiss on the lips.

"Time for breakfast."

Leaving the mess for their attendants to clean up, the pair donned matching black, silk dressing robes and made their way to the grand dining hall, where a table overloaded with food awaited them. One of the many perks of being married to the Devil was the ability to never ever have to exercise to work off his excesses.

Pure bliss.

Taking their places, the couple was served by shackled servants – televangelists who'd been a tad too greedy with their followers' money.

"Who do you feel like tormenting today?" asked Lucifer, as he helped himself to a generous serving of pumpkin cheesecake.

"How about some theatre critics?" suggested Gabriel with a malicious glee. "We can make them relive all of their failed acting endeavors and heckle them."

"Nice. Then perhaps we can visit your old friend, Reverend Jones? He's just had his memory wiped so he's all ready for some fresh Hell."

"Perfect. You really know how to spoil a guy, Angelboy"

"For you, my love, anything."

I guess it isn't all bad down here. Besides, I always did adore the heat.

GHOST OF A CHANCE

Levi Charleston looked up from his cooking and directed his gaze towards his husband, who was sitting in front of the fireplace and reading one of his favorite novels. It was such a cozy scene and Levi felt his lips forming a wide grin.

Damn, I love that man.

Strange to think, but if it hadn't been for a broken leg and a bout of food poisoning they may never have even gotten together, let alone ended up happily married. Given the circumstances, it had hardly been love at first sight but fate can be a funny thing. Indeed, Levi often marveled at how things worked out.

Even though it was mid-summer, the day had been decidedly miserable. It was unusually cold outside and the rain beat down in a relentless fashion, giving the impression of a constant sheet of water attempting to submerge the house. Even though he preferred the heat of the summertime, Levi wasn't too perturbed by the inclement weather.

Perfect day to be inside.

As the pots bubbled and steamed around him, Levi happily went about his pleasurable toil, humming to himself. Food was one of his most ardent passions, and luckily so was mountain biking, enabling him to work off all the tasty treats he concocted and consumed. His husband, Mitchell, hadn't been much of a cook when they first met but he'd slowly developed an interest through Levi's gentle encouragement. It helped that their cooking lessons tended to end up with one of them being fucked hard over the kitchen counter.

Best way to work up an appetite.

Finishing up, Levi opened the preheated oven and placed the vegetarian lasagna – it was Mitchell's favorite – on the middle tray. He closed the door and had to steady himself as a sudden wave of fatigue hit him. Catching his reflection in the shiny oven door, Levi noticed that his almond shaped eyes looked weary.

Early night tonight, I think.

Dinner wouldn't be ready for about an hour so Levi made himself a hot chocolate with a dash of Baileys liqueur to give it a bit of kick. Walking across to the fireplace, he sat down in the armchair opposite Mitchell. They often spent many hours in these chairs, reading and making the occasional comment to one another whenever something took their fancy. He cherished those quiet times, even though there was always a tinge of regret that their plans for a bigger family had never come to fruition.

All in all, it was shaping up to be a lovely evening for just the two of them. The driving rain was rather discouraging of visitors, after all. Settling into his chair, Levi picked up his copy of Misery from the small wooden table next to him and began to read – he did so love his regular dose of horror. As he began to lose himself in the story, Levi had the same thought that he'd had daily for the last two years.

If only Mitchell wasn't dead.

* * *

Twelve years beforehand, Levi was at something of a crossroads. His parents had perished in an avalanche whilst skiing in the French Alps, leaving him orphaned at the young age of twenty-two. Further adding to the sorrow, Levi had no siblings or other close relatives to help him deal with the hefty estate they'd left behind – it had been an overwhelming time to say the least. He didn't even have any close friends to turn to in his hour of need as his parents' emphasis on devoting all his time to studying had effectively killed Levi's social life before it had a chance to thrive.

Deferring his second year of legal studies, Levi spent a few months at the family home in The Hamptons sorting through their possessions. To be fair, he'd been having doubts about pursuing a legal profession, as it had always been more his parents' dream career for him than his own. Once or twice he'd raised the possibility of his becoming a restaurateur, but they'd always managed to talk him around to their way of thinking.

The vast majority of the estate was tied up in stocks and various investments that the family accountant, Mr. Seymour Dawes, had spent an extremely tedious afternoon trying to explain to him. He was a non-descript man in his late fifties with a monotone voice that had nearly caused Levi to nod off a few times during their meeting. Essentially, this meant that while waiting for the balance of his parents' bank accounts to be transferred over and for his trust fund to be released, he'd only have access to his own savings, which weren't exactly plentiful.

Feeling aimless, Levi was in desperate need of a break. Treating himself to a small two-week holiday, Levi chose to fly to the bustling city of Port Davinica, on the other side of the country, where he knew no one and nothing would be asked of him. He had dim but pleasant memories of the city from a trip with his maternal grandparents some years before. In keeping with his budget he had found reasonably priced accommodation on Airbnb. He would be sharing with the owner, Sara, but she'd already assured him that due to her work and social life she'd practically never be home. Not that this bothered Levi, as he planned on spending a good chunk of time exploring the city and seeing how his childhood recollections matched up to the modern reality.

After an uneventful flight and taxi ride to Sara's building, Levi found the right apartment and knocked on the solid-looking, wooden door. A minute or so passed and he knocked again. Then he heard a slight commotion inside, followed by a heavy dragging sound and quite a few profanities. The noise gradually approached the front door, which was yanked open with some vigor to reveal a disgruntled man, instead of the bright bubbly redhead he expected to find. Despite the man's disagreeable demeanor, he was strikingly handsome, with a muscular build, chocolate-brown eyes and chestnut curls atop his head. Looking down, Levi saw the man had a large cast on his right leg and now understood the noises.

"What do you want?" asked the man gruffly.

"Hi, I'm Levi. Ummm…I booked a room with Sara?"

"Ah, yeah. Right. I forgot you were coming today. I'm her brother, Mitchell. She isn't here, she's on the trip I should've been on if I hadn't broken my fucking leg."

The bitterness was radiating off of his potential host and Levi stood awkwardly on the doorstep. This was hardly the warm welcome he'd been expecting. While Levi thought Mitchell was attractive any libidinous thoughts he had were quickly dampened by his less than convivial attitude. Absentmindedly, Levi tugged on his left earlobe – a nervous habit he'd retained from childhood.

"Can I come in?" Levi asked timidly.

"Yeah, sure."

"Is it still, OK, that I stay? Sara didn't say anything in her messages."

"It was all a bit last minute. This only happened three days ago and she's been rushing around getting herself organized. She should have told you though."

"No, that's fine. As long as I won't be in your way."

"I'll survive," muttered Mitchell.

Levi searched for humor in the comment but wasn't able to discern any trace. Then his host hobbled down the hallway towards the lounge room where the television was blaring away with the sounds of a daytime soap opera.

"Umm…Where is my room?"

Mitchell stopped mid-shuffle, sighed and turned slightly.

"The first room on the right. The bathroom and the kitchen are on the other side of the lounge room. The spare keys are in the blue bowl by the door. Have a great stay."

This is off to a crappy start! It's fine. I hopefully won't be spending much time here anyway.

Determinedly ignoring the obvious lack of enthusiasm from his reluctant host, Levi put his bags away and headed back out to explore the city. Regrettably, his sightseeing was cut short by the sudden appearance of an electrical storm barely an hour after he'd left the apartment. He'd been strolling through Janeway Park – a huge expanse of greenery in the middle of the city – enjoying the scenery when the sun disappeared behind walls of dark grey clouds and a cold wind picked up. The first raindrops started to fall as he reached the south gates, so he took shelter in a nearby café, Perk Up, figuring he'd wait it out with a nice cup of hot chocolate and the novel he brought in his bag, just in case. Two hours later, the storm showed no signs of abating, buffeting the big glass windows of the café with wind and rain. Grudgingly, Levi booked an Uber and made his way back to the apartment. He wasn't looking forward to spending the rest of the day with his sullen new roommate.

I hope he's in a better mood, at least.

Unfortunately, he wasn't. Mitchell was lying on the couch where Levi had left him, staring blankly at the TV, with an aura of annoyance about him.

"I'm back," greeted Levi. "The weather didn't agree with my plans."

Mitchell gave a vague grunt of acknowledgement but his gaze didn't leave the flickering screen in front of him. Levi retired to his room, thankful that he'd brought a few Stephen King books along with him, to help while away the time.

The next day proved just as inclement. A cyclone up North had scattered all the good weather he'd been expecting and replaced it with grey skies and rain that varied from a drizzle to a downpour. The lackluster company wasn't helping matters and Levi was seriously considering just going back home and taking another holiday later. Giving himself to the following day to decide, Levi was happy to awaken to sun streaming through the curtains he hadn't closed properly the night before.

In high spirits, he set off early with a list of things to visit and his good mood wasn't even tainted by the morose Mitchell who appeared to have set up permanent camp on the sofa. Levi was fairly sure he slept there.

At least he must have showered 'cause he doesn't smell. Not that I'd want to smell him. Well...maybe if he wasn't so disagreeable.

After a fun day out seeing the sights and doing a spot of shopping in the gay district, Levi was feeling much more satisfied with his holiday destination. He quite enjoyed the eclectic architecture, particularly the gothic-inspired St James cathedral in the heart of the city. The fact that it was deconsecrated and had become a thriving gay nightclub also added to the appeal.

His self-esteem had certainly gotten a boost from the several appreciative glances he'd received whilst out and about. His athletic build, coupled with his dark golden skin and Eurasian features – courtesy of a Japanese father and American mother – attracted interest from men and women alike.

Following his day of sightseeing, he was ravenous and had planned to grab a bite on the way back but he hadn't passed anything to tempt his appetite. If he'd been at home, Levi would have stocked up at the supermarket and happily whipped up something himself but he was hesitant to use the kitchen lest it antagonize Mitchell further. Returning to the apartment, Levi saw a stack of menus sitting on the counter by the fridge but had no idea what might be good. Against his better judgment he thought to ask Mitchell's advice.

"Any recommendations for takeaway?" Levi asked, waving the menus.

Without tearing his eyes away from the screen, Mitchell answered unenthusiastically.

"Depends what you want. The closest is Cluck You at the end of the street. It's good for chicken and baked vegetables."

It was hardly a ringing endorsement but it did sound appetizing.

"Great. Thanks." In another attempt of friendliness he asked. "Did you want anything?"

"Nope."

"OK, then."

Twenty minutes later, Levi sat at the kitchen table wolfing down the recently delivered food. It was delicious but he'd only managed to get halfway through the food, as he'd ordered far too much.

No point offering Mitchell any, he'll just say no. Leftovers tomorrow, I guess.

After dinner, Levi settled into bed with one of his books and read for a little while before switching off the light and sinking into slumber, content from having his first enjoyable day since he arrived. Unhappily, the night did not bring the same satisfaction. Some hours later he was rudely awoken by severe stomach cramps. Blindly stumbling to the bathroom, Levi barely managed to sink to his knees in front of the toilet before violently throwing up his dinner.

After a few minutes there was a gentle rapping on the door.

"Levi, are you OK?"

"Not really, I…"

Yet another gut-wrenching spasm and the subsequent voiding of his stomach interrupted his sentence. This continued on and off for the next hour, until Levi literally had nothing left to give.

In an unanticipated show of compassion, Mitchell had brought Levi cold cloths and glasses of water to help make him more comfortable as his body fought to relieve itself of toxins. Catching sight of himself in the bathroom mirror, Levi was shocked to his see his reflection looking practically cadaverous.

I don't think I've ever been this sick.

Then Mitchell helped the severely weakened, and thoroughly grateful, Levi from the bathroom to the sofa. Levi noticed that Mitchell's belongings had been cleared away and in their place was fresh linen and a pillow.

How thoughtful. Maybe he isn't all that bad?

"It's better to rest here. Closer to the bathroom, but there's a bucket right by your head if you can't make it that far," explained Mitchell. "Do you think it was your dinner? I'm so sorry. I've never had any problems with them before."

"Not your fault," mumbled Levi.

"Are you sure you don't want me to call a doctor?"

"Nah, I think I'm over the worst of it."

"OK, but if you're still sick tomorrow you have no choice. My sister would kill me if you ended up dying. She wants to keep her high rating, after all."

Levi laughed and regretted it immediately, as his stomach muscles protested. On the bright side, the ice appeared to be broken between them. Despite his unfortunate state, Levi observed a look of great concern tinged with guilt upon Mitchell's countenance.

"Please just call out if you need anything," offered Mitchell, his tone positively friendly. "I'll leave my bedroom door open."

"Mitchell."

"Yes?"

"Thanks so much for looking after me."

"'Least I could do. Try and get some sleep."

Levi slept fitfully but mercifully there were no further violent gastric attacks. The following morning, he awoke feeling drained and still slightly nauseous. Mitchell hobbled about the apartment fetching Levi whatever he needed – mostly water, as it was all he could stomach. Throughout the day Levi drifted off for several naps, but whenever he woke up he noticed that Mitchell was never far away.

That evening, the cramps and nausea had subsided somewhat, so Mitchell gave Levi some rice crackers.

"I went down to Cluck You while you were sleeping this afternoon to let them know what had happened and have a go at them, but I was like the fifth person to tell them. Apparently the temperature gauge in one of their storage fridges broke and the chicken got too warm and voila…food poisoning. On the plus side they did give me a whole pack of free coupons."

"Not sure I'll be eating from there again," grumbled Levi. "They're all yours."

"Thanks, but I might steer clear of them for a while, too."

They sat in silence for a minute or two, watching the latest episode of Real Housewives of Belfast.

"Sorry that I've been such a jerk," apologized Mitchell out of the blue. "I was annoyed about missing my trip and took it out on you."

"I'll survive," murmured Levi, giving him a weak smile.

Over the next few days, the pair spent quite a deal of time together as Levi rested and slowly regained his strength. To Levi, it seemed like Mitchell had become a completely different person. Gone was the surly, petulant child and in his place was a man that Levi was enjoying getting to know. After chatting, they discovered they shared quite a few interests, including a mutual love of horror, especially schlocky eighties films.

That Friday, the twosome decided to hold a horror marathon with Freddy Kruger, Jason Voorhees and Michael Myers all putting in an appearance. They were seated rather close together on the sofa under an exceedingly soft wool blanket; the nights had been getting cooler. Their legs were pressed up comfortably together and they were sharing a large bowl of M&Ms, which allowed for quite a few 'accidental' touches as they ate.

I wouldn't mind if something happened but I don't want to make the first move. What if I'm reading things wrong and he kicks me out? Just enjoy the film.

By two in the morning they were both starting to become tired. Levi found himself closing his eyes for increasingly long periods, but trying to hold out for the end of the film before going to bed. After one such resting of his eyes, Levi suddenly woke with a start when one of the victims on the screen let out a particularly loud scream. It was then that he realized he'd actually fallen asleep on Mitchell's shoulder.

"Sorry," squirmed Levi, feeling embarrassed. "Hope I didn't drool on you."

"Nah, it's fine," replied Mitchell, with a warm smile. "It felt nice to be your pillow."

"Your shoulder is fairly comfy."

"So are other parts of me."

They looked at one another intensely, the attraction palpable. Very slowly, their faces came forward and their lips connected for a soft kiss. This quickly grew in passion as their hands began to roam under the blankets. As they kissed, Levi breathed in the pleasant citrus scent of Mitchell's cologne. Moving on top of Mitchell, the easiest position because of his cast, Levi continued to kiss his host with a growing desire. Their writhing bodies and increasingly loud moans of satisfaction eagerly proclaimed the mutual arousal.

Moving down Mitchell's body by means of a series of kisses, Levi came level with his host's crotch. He kissed all around the edge of the waistband of Mitchell's shorts, teasing the exposed skin with his tongue. Eventually he unbuttoned the fly and pulled the pants down to reveal obscenely bulging underwear, with a large damp spot where the cockhead strained against the material. Sucking and lightly biting the manhood through the underwear, Levi's hunger intensified. Unable to wait any longer, he pulled down the jocks, allowing seven uncut inches to bounce up into his face. His leg might be broken, but everything else was in fine working order.

Starting at the top, Levi hungrily licked the sticky cockhead, while nibbling on the foreskin. Then he ran his tongue along the length of the stiff shaft, lapping around the balls before coming back to the tip. Levi felt Mitchell's hands pressing into the back of his head as he started to go back down, slowly and tenderly moving his head in a corkscrew motion getting closer to the base which each bob. Soon, his face was buried in Mitchell's dark, trimmed hair, his fingers massaging the balls and rubbing the perineum, causing Mitchell to grunt and thrust forward.

"The bed will be easier," suggested Mitchell, after a few pleasurable minutes.

Levi helped Mitchell to the bedroom, where they discarded their clothes – it took a little effort to free Mitchell's shorts from his cast. Once naked they lay down on the bed together, kissing and caressing with great ardor. At Mitchell's urging, Levi sat astride his host's chest and placed his manhood into the invitingly warm mouth. Wasting no time, Mitchell teased the foreskin briefly before devouring it to the base. Using the wall for leverage, Levi pumped his cock into Mitchell's face, his balls bouncing off of his stubbly chin. The deep-throating felt amazing, but Levi knew he wouldn't last too much longer and there was something else he was hankering for first.

"Condoms?" asked Levi, once he'd removed the impediment to Mitchell answering.

"Bottom drawer," instructed Mitchell.

It only took a few moments for Levi to locate and use the necessary supplies. Once ready, Levi straddled Mitchell's hips, lowering himself down onto the erect member. He gasped as his ring stretched to accommodate the fat mushroom head. It had been a while since he'd been fucked so Levi took it slow, lifting himself up and down in small movements, gradually taking inch after inch. For his part, Mitchell seemed content to let Levi take the lead. Leaning forward, Levi kissed Mitchell, the tongues lazily dueling as their bodies moved together in a slow sensual rhythm.

After his passageway had fully adjusted to the intruder, Levi began to rise up and slam back down, feeling the manhood hit deep inside him with every thrust, causing electric shocks of pleasure. As he bounced up and down his own cock swung wildly in front of him leaving droplets of precum over Mitchell's straining body. The bed creaked in response to the increased intensity of their play and the air in the room became heated and heavily fragranced with the heady musk of their combined perspiration.

In desperate need of release, Levi started to jack himself at a furious pace. Only a few minutes later he could feel his balls churning with a well-earned load. Grunting, Levi squeezed his ass muscles as his cockhead erupted and rained his seed over Mitchell's chest. It was a sizeable load, as he hadn't cum since he'd been sick, and the white cream easily covered Mitchell's erect, cocoa-brown nipples before slowly dripping down the sides of his firm chest.

As Levi moved forward to kiss Mitchell, the manhood slipped free of the warm embrace of his channel. Reaching around, Mitchell ripped off the condom and wanked himself, obviously keen for his own happy ending. Within a handful of strokes his body shuddered and Mitchell ejaculated all over Levi's lower back, which then gently trickled down over his ass cheeks. They kept kissing tenderly as their breathing and heartbeats returned to normal.

"Damn that was hot," declared Mitchell, a huge grin upon his face. "And to think we could have been doing that all week."

"Yeah, if you hadn't been such a jerk," teased Levi.

"You're here for another week, aren't you?"

"Why yes, yes I am."

No further conversation was needed as their lips reconnected in an amorous embrace. Predictably, it wasn't long before their restored erections began to insist on further play. Rolling awkwardly onto his stomach, the cast impeding his mobility, Mitchell made it quite clear what he expected from Levi. Not one to refuse such a kind request, Levi quickly suited up and slid himself into Mitchell's pleasingly tight passageway. Mitchell groaned as Levi's seven fat inches forced their way inside, probing deep and possessing the channel. Once he was in to the hilt, Levi kissed the back of Mitchell's neck as he lovingly ground into the warm tunnel. With the pressing need for release already satiated, neither of the pair was in a hurry, happy to draw out their coupling for as long as possible. Keeping to the same position to avoid issues with the cast, Levi made tender love to Mitchell. Taking his time, Levi slid himself in and out, long-dicking Mitchell, while he ran his hands along his host's squirming body. Roughly an hour later, their exquisite leisurely play culminated in another round of orgasms.

That night, Levi fell asleep spooning Mitchell in his bed – something which became the norm every night for the rest of his stay. Needless to say, Levi didn't see much of the city over the following week with his time spent either in Mitchell's bed or cuddled up next to him on the couch – not that he minded the unexpected turn of events in the slightest.

Indeed, the whole situation began to feel worryingly comfortable and Levi found that he wasn't looking forward to leaving. All too soon, the last night arrived and to mark the occasion, the pair enjoyed a candlelit dinner, lovingly prepared by Levi, and a nice bottle of wine followed by another round of lovemaking. As they lay together, holding one another in hazy afterglow of their fucking, Levi felt safe, secure and happy.

I don't ever want to leave.

"Please stay," whispered Mitchell between kisses.

"I wish I could," murmured Levi. "But I have things to sort out at home."

"Then promise me you'll come back."

"I promise."

Drifting off to sleep, wrapped up in Mitchell's arms, Levi only had one thought on repeat.

Could this be my fresh start?

* * *

The following morning there was a tear-filled goodbye – after enjoying one last energetic bout of passionate play. The emotion was running high on both sides and Levi once again renewed his promise to return in the not too distant future. Mitchell offered to go to the airport with him but Levi opted for a more private farewell. On the flight home, Levi dwelled on his time with Mitchell and where his life was headed.

Time to move on. To Port Davinica? Why not? There's nothing for me in The Hamptons. Yeah, but moving to a city for a guy I just met? Would he even want me to? What if it doesn't work out? What if it does?

As soon as he landed, Levi called Mitchell.

"Hey Mister, how was the flight?" asked Mitchell with a forced cheerfulness.

"It was good. It gave me chance to have a bit of a think. How would you feel about my coming back to Port Davinica?

"You know I want you to come back," affirmed Mitchell. "I thought I proved that again this morning."

"You certainly did. I mean...would it be OK if I came for a longer time?"

"You don't need my permission, doofus. Why how long were you thinking?"

Here goes. I hope he doesn't freak out.

"Permanently?" said Levi in a half-whisper.

"I think that'd be awesome...but are you sure? You aren't just coming for me are you? Don't get me wrong I am pretty amazing sex but I wouldn't want you making any rash decisions."

"Ha! Trust me, as wonderful as your body parts are, that isn't the whole reason. In truth, I need a fresh start and I think Port Davinica is as good a place as any. It won't be straight away as it will take a little while to sort things out here, but I should be able to be back in a month or so. I know this is all kind of sudden but this last week with you has been so great and I think that maybe it could lead somewhere. What do you think?"

"I think that I can't wait till you're back!"

Feeling much relieved, Levi gathered his luggage from the carousel and jumped into a taxi. Returning to the family home, Levi began to make the preparations necessary for him to uproot his life. Several days, and a good many phone calls and emails later, his plans were very much in motion. The house would be listed on the market and all the furnishings he'd opted to keep were going to be shipped to a storage facility until he had a new address. His trust fund would be released to him at the end of the month, at which point he would be free to buy a new house.

The duo kept in daily contact with multiple texts, photos and regular video chats to keep the flames of their passion well and truly stoked. Six weeks later, when everything was finally sorted, Levi hopped back on the plane and was met at the airport by a fully healed Mitchell. Upon reaching the apartment they wasted no time stripping off and engaging in some very athletic sex now that Mitchell's physical limitation was no more.

Emerging from the bedroom for a much-needed water break, Levi ran right into a petit blue-eyed woman with a mess of auburn curls coming down the hallway. Fortunately, he'd wrapped himself in a towel before exiting.

"Sara?" guessed Levi.

"And you must be Levi! It's so good to finally meet you," gushed Sara exuding friendliness. "It looks like things worked out well on your stay, then."

"Yeah, you could say that."

"Mitchell says you're moving here for good. It must be so exciting starting over in a new city! I don't know if I could do it but good on you for following your heart. Have you found a new place yet? Of course, you're welcome to stay here for as long as you like."

"Sara," called the disembodied voice of Mitchell from the bedroom. "Stop interrogating my boyfriend."

"Well, don't mind me. I just popped home to change. You get back to…whatever you were doing. Bye."

"Thanks, I will."

Returning to the bedroom with two glasses of water, Levi gave Mitchell a broad smile.

"Now, where were we?"

Their reunion continued into the early hours until they both fell asleep from exhaustion, their bodies well and truly reacquainted.

Happily, Levi's leap of faith was well rewarded and hardly a year later he was standing on a white sandy beach in Hawaii, exchanging vows in front of a select few family and friends.

"Mitchell, you've opened up your whole world to me and made me feel so welcome and loved. I really feel like I've found another family and for that I'm truly grateful. I can't wait to spend the rest of my life with you."

The ceremony was followed by a rollicking celebration filled with a good many tears and laughter. Mitchell's family had warmed to Levi immediately and readily accepted him as one of their own without even the slightest objection to their whirlwind romance. Indeed, Mitchell's sisters, Sara and Nathalie, often jokingly remarked how much they preferred Levi as a brother than Mitchell.

The pair spent the next two weeks honeymooning at a luxury resort on Kauai, before returning to Port Davinica. Coming home they moved straight into a townhouse right in the heart of the gayborhood that Levi had bought Mitchell as a wedding present. They even took turns carrying each over the threshold.

Life doesn't get much better than this.

* * *

Five years passed by and life was going along rather swimmingly for Levi. In addition to being happily married to a kind and handsome man, he was also the proud owner of The Spicy Samurai – a Mexican-Japanese fusion restaurant he'd started with his business partner and closest friend Corey Duncan. In his early forties, Corey was as passionate about food as Levi, something quite evident in his rotund physique. They'd met at a food fair not long after Levi had moved to Port Davinica, where they'd both been captivated by a truffle-centric stall and had been fast friends ever since. The restaurant had been an instant success and they'd since expanded into the shop next door and now had a large terrace area for the warmer months. Part of their popularity was their ever-changing menu – Levi adored experimenting with new combinations. Naturally, there'd been a few disasters that had never made it past the trial stage – sashimi nachos, for instance – but for the most part Levi's creativity was rewarded with delectable victories.

Even though his professional and personal lives were fantastic, Levi felt the pull for something more – namely children. His desire for offspring of his own was partly driven by Mitchell's family, particularly his niece and nephew.

These days, Sara lived in New Zealand and operated a scuba-diving school with her tanned, blond surfer husband, Dean Sanders. Their adorable little four-year-old, Gigi, was the spitting image of her mother. Levi's heart melted whenever they Skyped with them and Gigi proudly informed them of what she'd been up to in preschool.

Mitchell's older sister, Nathalie, a curvaceous, brunette realtor, still resided in Port Davinica and was married to Martin

Fairchild, a kindhearted man with thinning raven hair and the beginnings of a middle-age spread. Their teenage son Patrick, a good-looking athletic lad with honey-blond hair and emerald-green eyes, was a frequent visitor to Levi and Mitchell's townhouse. They'd become very close with Patrick over the past few years, so much so that when he was questioning his sexuality it was Levi and Mitchell he'd confided in first. They provided a sounding board until he officially came out a few months later, not that his parents were perturbed by the news. The pair continued to answer Patrick's many, many questions about gay life, especially the dating and sex parts, which his parents weren't particularly well-versed in.

"So, are all gay guys into fisting?" Patrick blurted out one evening at dinner with just the three of them.

"And, I'm out," declared Mitchell. "Vi, you can handle all further questions."

"Don't be such a prude," admonished Levi.

"Hey, just because I don't believe men should be used as puppets doesn't mean I'm a prude," quipped Mitchell defensively.

"Is it something you're interested in Patrick?" continued Levi.

"Well, not really but I see so much of it in porn. I mean all the other stuff looks really hot but I was unsure about that."

"Some guys are into that type of play but it's not for everyone. Don't worry, you have plenty of time to find out whether or not it's something you're…into. Personally, it doesn't appeal to me but I tend to be non-judgmental on the private consensual habits of others…unlike some."

"Pffft," said Mitchell with a playful smile.

Mitchell's parents, Frank and Nancy, had also stoked Levi's paternal longings, raising the subject of more grandchildren at every opportunity without a great deal of subtlety. As was the case when they had Levi and Mitchell over for a Sunday roast dinner.

"It's such a shame that Gigi is so far away," lamented Frank, a heavyset man with steel-gray eyes and salt and pepper hair. "Video chats just aren't the same."

"Yes, and with Mitchell nearly grown up, I really miss having little ones about the place," added Nancy, a fine figure of a woman with clear blue eyes and perfectly coiffed auburn curls.

"Just think of all the spare time you have," teased Mitchell, knowing very well what his parents were heavily hinting at.

Later that night, Levi and Mitchell were lying in bed and discussing the possibility of adding to their family unit.

"How many?" exclaimed Mitchell, after Levi had given him a rather shocking number.

"OK, fine. Maybe not seven then…how about five?" grinned Levi. "Alright, three! And that's my final offer."

"We're haggling now? How about we start with one and see where we go from there."

"Spoilsport, you're no fun!"

"I prefer the term realist."

"There's just so many needy kids waiting to be adopted and I know we can offer a loving home. I see your family and how close they all are and I just want that for us…and a baby…or a dozen."

"Vi!"

"Joking…kind of."

Of course, once they'd decided to take the leap into the world of adoption it was hefty chunk of time before their dream of fatherhood looked like becoming a reality – three years to be exact. After signing up with Forever Families, an agency that specialized in helping gay couples, every last facet of their lives was dug into as they had countless meetings with a variety of professionals – doctors, social workers and psychologists. Guiding them through the harrowing process was their caseworker, Miriam Daniels, a corpulent lady in her late fifties, with friendly mud-brown eyes and frizzy brunette hair.

Eventually, they were matched with an African-American girl, Delilah, who was nearly three years old. She'd been in the foster system for most of her life after being removed from her mother for neglect. Her father was currently serving time in prison for a botched bank robbery. From the first moment they saw the mocha-skinned girl with her beautiful dark eyes and wide smile, the couple was smitten. After a friendly introduction to her, they'd had a few supervised visits, after which Levi and Mitchell were truly besotted.

Everything was proceeding on schedule and they'd even decorated a room for her, filling it with an abundance of toys, books and colorful posters. Their excitement built as the date neared for the final paperwork and Levi felt like he was constantly beaming with happiness at the prospect of finally being a dad.

Lamentably, their hope and joy came crashing down two days before they were to sign the paperwork finalizing the adoption when Miriam called them in for an unscheduled meeting.

"It's bad news I'm afraid. The adoption is on hold," explained Miriam, clearly disappointed. "Delilah's paternal grandparents have filed for custody."

"Where the hell have they been then?" demanded Levi furiously. "Where were they when her mother was leaving her in soiled nappies for days on end while she went off on benders? And fine job they did with their own son that ended up a criminal. Why the Hell are they only interested now?"

"Please, Levi. I know that this is difficult for you both and I understand your anger but they only just became aware of her existence and are very keen to have her."

"Is there anything we can do?" asked Mitchell, clearly devastated. "Can't we put in an injunction of our own or something?

"You could take this to court, but to be perfectly frank the judges do tend to side with keeping the child with the biological family if they can provide for the child."

"So, what now?" insisted Levi. "Can we see her?"

"No, for the moment, it's probably best to see how things go with the grandparents petition."

They returned home in a very somber mood, neither talking much about what had transpired. Levi drowned his sorrows in a few lethally strong gin and tonics and began to brood in earnest. Later that evening, Mitchell found his husband radiating despair while standing in the room they'd prepared for Delilah.

"This is bullshit!" shouted Levi.

"I know, Vi, but there's nothing we can do," comforted Mitchell, taking Levi into his arms. "Trust me, I'm just as angry and upset as you are."

"We would've made amazing parents for her."

"I know," whispered Mitchell, silent tears rolling down his cheeks.

That night, the pair had held each other in bed, both utterly miserable but taking comfort in each other's presence. It took hours before Levi was able to drift off to sleep, as his mind kept moving between sorrow, rage and futility.

Why? This is so damn unfair. We just want to be Dads!

* * *

Sadly, they didn't see Delilah again, as the judge granted her grandparents' petition. The day they found out, Levi was inconsolable. He blew off work and spent the day in a state of maudlin drunkenness. Mitchell took it equally badly but followed the opposite approach and began to spend even longer days at his brokerage firm, losing himself in a bustle of share-trading and pension funds.

Unsurprisingly, their markedly different coping mechanisms and the stress of the adoption falling through led to a rough patch between the pair. A few weeks later, Levi was keen to try again but Mitchell was far more reluctant, obviously not ready to put himself through the emotional process again so quickly. As a result, they found that they were beginning to snipe at one another over trivial matters. Even getting into a mini-screaming match over whose turn it had been to pick up some milk on the way home from work. The instability had been ongoing for nearly two months when things came to a head.

Coming home from the restaurant one evening, Levi found that Mitchell had packed up everything in Delilah's room into boxes, leaving the space looking desolate.

What the fuck? How could he?

"What did you do?" shouted Levi, his voice full of fury.

"Don't yell at me," responded Mitchell defensively. "I couldn't bear to look at it any more. It was breaking my heart every time I walked past the doorway."

"Don't you want kids anymore?"

"Of course I damn well do. You know that. It's just been exhausting emotionally and I need some time to process it all."

"But we aren't getting any younger," argued Levi. "I don't want to let so much time go by that we miss out altogether."

"I'm sorry, I just can't right now. I need space and time to think."

"Think about what exactly?" questioned Levi suspiciously.

"Look we've been fighting a lot lately and I think it may be a good idea if…we spent some time apart. I'm going to stay at Nathalie and Martin's for a few days to help clear my head."

It was then that Levi noticed one of their suitcases standing in the hallway.

I can't lose him too! Not after everything else. He's the only family I have.

"Please don't go. Don't leave me," pleaded Levi, tears starting to prick his eyes. "I know we can work this out together."

"I need to do this for both our sakes. We can't keep on going like this. I love you, I do, but I'm afraid that we won't be able to get back to how we used to be if we don't take a break. I hate fighting all the time. I'm exhausted by it, Vi. Aren't you?"

Standing there, Levi couldn't find the words to answer. Part of him knew that Mitchell was right but his fear of losing everything kept him from accepting it.

"Please, Mitchell. I'll do anything you want," begged Levi. "I can't do this alone."

"I'm sorry, Levi," murmured Mitchell, as he turned and grabbed his suitcase. "I'll call you later."

Levi stood in place until he heard the front door close behind his husband, which is when he broke down and fell to the floor in tears. His sobbing echoed through their townhouse and made Levi feel even lonelier. He vaguely thought of calling Corey but he didn't want to admit to himself, let alone anyone else, what had happened with Mitchell.

I've failed. I'm going to lose everything.

A very tough two weeks followed and communication between them was minimal at best. At work, Levi put on a brave face but when he came home he turned to the bottle for comfort. His drinking began to steadily increase and looked well on the way to becoming problematic when Mitchell unexpectedly threw Levi a lifeline with a late-night phone call.

"Hi, sorry to bother you so late, but I've been feeling so distant from you and I hate it. I wanted to hear your voice. To be honest, I'm pretty fucking miserable."

"Me too," admitted Levi. "Please come home."

"I'm not quite ready for that but would you be willing to try counseling?" offered Mitchell.

"Yes, of course," agreed Levi enthusiastically. "Whatever it takes. I don't want to lose you."

"You haven't lost me," reassured Mitchell. "We just need to do some work on our relationship. I still love you."

For the first time since the adoption had fallen through, Levi felt truly hopeful.

We can start again.

A month later, they were sat together on a large blue sofa in the comfortable office of Dr. Evelyn Waters for their third appointment. The first two sessions had been dedicated to getting the pair to a point where they could move past their anger and frustration, and be able to talk without fighting.

"Why do you feel the need to rush right into the adoptive process again, Levi?" inquired Dr. Waters, a capable woman in late sixties, with cascading grey hair and sharp blue eyes.

"Well…we're getting older and I don't want to be a grandpa chasing a toddler around."

"I think that's quite a long way off, just yet. Could it perhaps have more to do with your own family situation?"

"What do you mean?" asked Levi a tad defensively.

"You did lose your parents and have no other close relatives bar Mitchell's family. Perhaps you're afraid that if you don't cement the marriage with children that you may lose that family as well."

"I suppose…sometimes I do feel that it could all be taken away from me again," admitted Levi reluctantly.

"Vi, why didn't you tell me?" interjected Mitchell.

"I was afraid that if I said something it would put even more stress on us."

"Kids or not, you're not going to lose me, and you know my family would probably prefer you to me any way," joked Mitchell, a gentle grin lighting his face. "It's not that I don't want to try again, I just need to prepare myself."

"Would you be prepared to revisit the issue in say, six months?" asked Dr. Waters, steering the conversation back.

"Yes, I would," stated Mitchell with certainty. "How does that sound, Vi?"

"I think I can live with that," agreed Levi, giving his husband a small smile.

They were slowly making progress but Levi realized that they still had a way to go. Within a month, Mitchell had moved back in and they continued to work on their relationship, both being much more open and honest about their feelings. Not to say it was all plain sailing, and they still had the occasional squabble, but for the most part that were well on track to saving their marriage and their future together.

* * *

Several months passed and the pair did begin discussing the prospect of having children again. Just over a year after the first adoption fell through, they contacted Miriam and set up an appointment to start the process once more.

"I'm so glad to see you both again," greeted Miriam. "The good news is that the administration side will be a lot faster as we already have all your documentation. There will need to be new appointment with one of our counselors because of what happened last time but it should all be fine. Do you have any questions?"

"How long do you think it will it be before we're matched again," asked Levi.

"Well, there are quite a few children awaiting placement that may be a good match for you two, but we'll have a better idea in a month or so."

"That's fine, we'll be ready when you guys are," remarked Mitchell, smiling at Levi.

On the car ride home, Levi was struck by an idea.

"It's coming up to our tenth anniversary, why don't we have a second honeymoon? We can both take some time off and go to the beach house for a few weeks, while we're waiting for Forever Families to do their thing. What do you think?"

"I think that sounds like an awesome plan," agreed Mitchell. "We probably won't get a chance for a while afterwards."

And so, the following Friday, Levi left early in the morning and drove up the coast to their holiday home, leaving Mitchell to finish up a few things at his office. The pair had bought the house two years previously and rented it out when they weren't up there for the occasional long weekend or a few weeks during the summer. The area was sparsely populated so the beach was fairly private and the view unsullied by housing development.

Levi had finished preparing the dinner and was sitting on the back deck with a book and a large glass of rosé, when he realized that it was starting to get late. He'd spoken with Mitchell earlier, who'd promised Levi that he'd leave before peak hour. Feeling a niggling sense of worry, he tried Mitchell's phone a few times but it went straight to voicemail.

Probably just a lot of traffic leaving the city and he forgot to charge his phone again. Well, it'll be his fault if the lamb is overcooked.

As Levi went inside and switched the oven to low to keep the food warm, there was a sudden loud knocking on the door.

Finally!

"Didn't you bring your keys?" Levi called out as he went to answer the knock.

Opening the door, Levi was confronted with the unexpected sight of a policeman and policewoman both with somber expressions on their faces.

"Yes, can I help you?" inquired Levi his curiosity peaked.

"I'm looking for Mr. Levi Charleston," stated the policeman.

"That's me. How can I help you?"

"I'm Officer Brady and this is Officer Partridge. Is there anyone here with you?"

"No, but my husband should be arriving shortly. What is this about, officer?"

The officer shifted uncomfortably on the stoop, noticeably uneasy with the task at hand, he and his partner exchanged stony glances. Levi got an odd sensation in the pit of his stomach, as the impression that something was very wrong grew in intensity.

"Maybe it's best if we talked inside," offered the policewoman.

"No, please just tell me what's happening," insisted Levi, feeling anxious and scared.

"I'm very sorry to have to inform you that at 5.20pm this evening your husband was involved in an automobile accident. He was taken to hospital but... unfortunately he was declared deceased upon arrival."

No. No. No. No. No. No.

The world began to fall away and it was only due to the quick reflexes of the two officers that Levi didn't crash into the floor. They helped Levi to the sofa and the policewoman found her way to the kitchen and got him a glass of water.

"No, it can't be...I was talking to him on the phone only a few hours ago," said Levi in an increasingly agitated state. "How do you know? Are you really sure? I mean mistakes happen all the time. Please tell me it's not him."

"We were able to identify the bo...your husband from his driver's license. I'm sorry but there hasn't been a mistake," explained Officer Brady, with a softer tone. "A formal identification will need to be made but that can wait for the moment. Is there anyone we can call for you?"

"Where is he?" demanded Levi, shooting to his feet. "I want to see him! I need to make sure that it's him."

"I don't believe that would be a good idea, Mr. Charleston," counseled Officer Partridge. "The accident was quite...*severe* and it wouldn't be good to see him like that. Best wait until they've had a chance to make him presentable."

"Presentable? I can't...his family...I need to call his sisters. I should...but I don't...please tell me he's not dead..."

He collapsed in a flood of tears, his body wracked with sobbing. Eventually, the officers were able to get Corey's number from Levi. They stayed with him for over an hour until Corey, who'd immediately closed the restaurant, arrived to look after him.

"Anything you need, I'm here," reassured Corey, as he sat beside Levi on the sofa, his own eyes clouded with tears.

Levi barely acknowledged his best friend and was absolutely lost in his grief.

But we were starting again. I can't believe he's gone. I wish I were dead, too! I can't live without him.

* * *

Following the accident, Levi shut himself away at the beach house, hardly showering or eating for nearly three months and practically living in his white terry toweling dressing gown. He couldn't bear the thought of returning to the townhouse and being surrounded by the remnants of their life together. There were days when he couldn't even get out of bed and had seriously thought about ending it all but the thought of Mitchell's disapproval kept him from doing anything drastic.

He'd never forgive me if I did that to his family.

The only positive thing to come from his bereavement was that Levi had become even closer with his in-laws. It was their help, and Corey's of course, that had seen him through the dark days and forced him to take the minimum amount of care for himself.

Eventually, his depression began to lift and most days he almost felt like himself again, although never a day went by when he didn't think of Mitchell. It didn't help that there were reminders everywhere he looked, especially his platinum wedding band, which he was unable to even contemplate taking off.

I don't think I'll ever be ready.

Ever so slowly, Levi transformed back from the unhealthily thin, sallow-skinned and greasy-haired shell of a man back into his regular self. Still, Levi struggled to find joy in the world. While Levi was still co-owner of The Spicy Samurai he hadn't cooked there since before the accident – his zeal for food severely diminished. Fortunately, Corey had successfully kept things running in his absence.

That wasn't the only passion that had been dimmed by his husband's death. No other man had touched him intimately since Mitchell and he had no plans to start dating in the immediate future. Around a year after he'd become a widower,

Levi had gone to The Cat's Meow with Nathalie and some mutual friends, and had been having a lovely time until one of the barmen started flirting with him. He politely excused himself and then spent half an hour crying in the toilets.

It feels like I'm cheating on Mitchell.

Since then, his hand and pornography had serviced his carnal needs without the need for guilt.

Several months later Levi found himself growing restless. He was beginning to feel like he'd never be able to resume his old life fully. The idea of selling his share of the restaurant and perhaps starting anew in another city was growing in appeal.

But am I just going to run away to somewhere new every time I lose someone I love?

His indecision wasn't helped by the fact that Levi was waking each morning feeling tired no matter how much sleep he'd had the night before. This was on top of dull headaches that didn't ever really seem to go away and the occasional dizzy spell that lasted for a couple of seconds before he regained his balance. He'd been feeling out-of-sorts for nearly a month and vaguely contemplated seeing a doctor.

Maybe I need glasses. Or I'm coming down with something?

Walking into the kitchen one morning, Levi went to switch on the percolator to get his much-needed hit of caffeine when he stopped dead in his tracks, certain he must be dreaming. In the lounge room, sitting in an armchair reading was Mitchell, dressed in his navy-blue work suit and looking very much alive.

It can't be. Have I lost the plot?

"Mitchell?" asked Levi tentatively.

"Vi!" exclaimed Mitchell leaping up from the armchair. "You can see me?"

Rushing towards to the fireplace, Levi reached out to touch Mitchell but his hand went straight through to the armrest of the chair.

"Oh, sorry about that. I'm a ghost," explained Mitchell, his eyes heavy with sadness. "I thought you knew."

I knew it was too good to be true.

"Where have you been?" demanded Levi, his disappointment turning to anger. "Why are you only here now? I've needed you so much. It's been so awful without you."

"I've been here ever since I died. I tried to tell you I was still around but you couldn't see or hear me. It was Hell watching you and not being to comfort you…or my family. I don't know why you can only see me now, but I'm so glad that you can."

Hold on a sec.

"I haven't died, have I?" asked Levi warily.

"No, you're most definitely in the land of the living, my sweet, otherwise we could touch."

"Oh…well, it's still good to see you."

"You too, Vi."

They spent hours chatting just like they used to and while he couldn't touch his husband, Levi felt the happiest he'd been in years.

A few days later, Nathalie came by for their regular Saturday afternoon coffee and catch-up. At first Levi was tempted to cancel, as he didn't want anything to interrupt his and Mitchell's time together, but he was also curious to see if anyone else was privy to the ghostly interactions. After he'd led

Nathalie into the lounge room, Levi eagerly watched her expression. When there was no marked change he decided to prod a little.

"Notice anything different?" asked Levi, gesturing towards Mitchell who was sitting in a chair watching on with amusement.

"New curtains?" guessed Nathalie.

"No. There's not something *unusual*?" hinted Levi. "Out of the ordinary?"

"Oh my GOD! I can't believe it!"

Can she see him too? Great, I'm not going crazy.

"You've been baking! I can smell it. It makes me so happy that you're back in the kitchen."

"NO!" yelled Levi in frustration. "Sorry, I mean, yes I have been baking. I made some pumpkin scones for us to eat this afternoon. But that's not what I meant."

"Are you feeling alright? You seem a little *off* and look really tired." She'd always been rather plainspoken, it was one of the things that he admired about her. "Are you getting enough sleep?"

I guess it's just me then.

"Gee thanks. You look horrible too," jeered Levi lightheartedly. "Always such a delight to have you over."

"You know that's not what I meant."

"Actually, I have been having some headaches and the occasional dizzy spell and…"

Pausing, Levi debated the wisdom of telling Nathalie about seeing Mitchell.

She wouldn't believe me and I don't need any more pity. But she might?

"Yes?"

"You've been sick?" questioned Mitchell. "Why didn't you say anything?"

Ignoring Mitchell, Levi decided against disclosing his brush with the supernatural.

"And I'm just really tired all the time."

"It doesn't sound good at all. Go see a doctor. It might be stress but you need to make sure. Have you been worrying about anything in particular lately? You know I think you need to care of yourself better."

"Yes, Mom," mocked Levi laughing.

"That's enough lip out of you, Mister. I'm going to stand right here until you make an appointment."

"You better do what she says, she's a tyrant when she doesn't get her way," quipped Mitchell.

"Don't I know it," agreed Levi smiling.

"What?" asked Nathalie.

"Nothing, I'll call now."

Dutifully, he called his GP, Dr. Madeline Hastings, and made an appointment for the following Wednesday. Hanging up the phone, he turned back to his sister-in-law with a smug face.

"Happy now?"

"Immensely. So, when are you coming by for dinner? I know that Martin and Patrick would love to see you. It's been a little while."

"I know. I know. I've just been a little anti-social lately. Had a lot on my mind."

"Everything OK?"

"Nothing I can't handle," assured Levi. "How about tomorrow night?"

"Sounds good. Round eight?"

"Perfect! Can't wait."

"Wonderful. Now where are those scones I was promised?"

They sat at the small wooden table out of the back deck, enjoying a leisurely conversation while they drank coffee and munched on the scones, although Levi couldn't help sneaking the occasional glance towards Mitchell whenever Nathalie wasn't looking. After she left, Levi went back to the lounge room where Mitchell was standing with a serious look on his face.

"Why didn't you tell me you weren't feeling well?" insisted Mitchell, looking very cross.

"Oh, don't you start too."

"I may be dead, but I still love you, doofus."

"I know. Anyway, your sister already bullied me into going to the doctor so everyone can get off my back."

"Fine…for now. What did you want to do tonight? Watch a movie?"

"Sounds good to me."

This is almost as good as it was before…almost.

* * *

At the appointment, Levi described his symptoms but Dr. Hastings didn't appear overly concerned. She was a strikingly beautiful woman, who looked like she belonged on the catwalk rather than in a physician's office, with piercing grey eyes, midnight black hair down to her waist and a stunning figure many would happily kill for.

"It could be stress or possibly something a little more serious," advised Dr. Hastings. "I'd like to send you off for some blood tests and scans."

Three days later, Levi got a voicemail from the doctor's office encouraging him to make the earliest appointment he could. He called back and they squeezed him in the following morning.

"Do you want me to come with you?" asked Mitchell with concern.

"No, I might talk to you by mistake and then they'll lock me up for being delusional. Don't worry, I'm sure it's nothing too bad."

Once seated in front of the good doctor, Levi gathered that the results were not good. Instead of her usual smiley demeanor, her face was clouded with a sadness that Levi feared was very much to do with his condition.

"I'm afraid it's bad news, Levi. The cat scan detected a large mass in your frontal lobe. That's what been causing the headaches and dizziness. Sometimes it can also lead to hallucinations."

So it isn't really him...but I don't want the visions to stop.

"Cancer?" he asked with a wavering voice.

"Yes, and it appears to be highly aggressive for your symptoms to develop so quickly."

Fuck! What on earth did I do to deserve this kind of karma? I'm a good person, aren't I?

"So...umm...how do we treat it?"

"Unfortunately, due to its size and location it's inoperable. We can try chemotherapy to slow its progress and possibly shrink it to buy you some more time. My concern though is that it would also greatly deteriorate your quality of life without the guarantee of success. Personally, I'd advise against it."

It took a moment for her words to sink in and Levi was hit with the unpleasant reality of his situation.

Does she mean that...I'm dying?

"Sorry, are you saying that it's terminal no matter what I do?"

"Yes," replied Dr. Hastings, her watery eyes betraying her emotions.

But I'm only thirty-four! There's so much more I wanted to do. What the fuck?

"If...umm...I...ah..." Levi struggled to form a sentence as he tried to comprehend his unexpected diagnosis. "I'm not..."

"It's OK. Please take your time. This is a lot to process, especially after what you've been through these past few years. I can't tell you how truly sorry I am."

"How...how long do I have?" inquired Levi, his voice quavering even more.

"We can't say with certainty, as the growth rates vary, but given how aggressive it's shown itself to be my best guess would be six months to a year. Of course, I'll refer you to a neurologist who will be able to guide you through everything. I'm so sorry, Levi."

"Yeah, me too."

Shaken, Levi left the clinic and got into his car, where he just sat in the parking lot and stared at nothing. He didn't call anyone. He didn't even have the words to express his complete and utter hate for the pure injustice of it all.

Fuck this universe!

After an hour or so Levi returned home, although he didn't remember a minute of the drive there. Once inside, he went straight to the kitchen and poured himself a gin and tonic – minus the tonic.

"What's wrong?" questioned Mitchell upon seeing Levi's distressed state. "What did the doctor say?"

"Well, I'm just dandy. Apparently, the reason I can see you is due to this lovely brain tumor thing that's going to kill me in less than a year. So, there's that." In a fit of rage, Levi threw his glass hard against the wall, shattering it all over the tiled kitchen floor. "Haven't I suffered enough? My parents...you...if there is a God up there he can just fuck off!"

"Vi, I'm so sorry," said Mitchell, visibly upset. "Is there nothing they can do?"

"Chemo that may or may not do anything and will certainly make the rest of what little life I have left absolutely miserable."

"As much as I would love to hold you in my arms. I'd rather you live. Surely the chemo is worth it if it can give you more time?"

"And die as a bald, frail man, sick to my stomach and a shell of what I was? No thanks. Now, if you don't mind, I'm going to drink myself into a stupor."

True to his word, Levi then proceeded to make himself another drink, ignoring the mess on the floor. He then proceeded to consume anything alcoholic he could find in the house until he passed out in a depressed daze.

* * *

After the neurologist, Dr. Theo Stevens, confirmed the initial diagnosis, the next month passed by in a blur of doctors' appointments. Levi consulted with him and Dr. Hastings but declined the see the counselor they'd recommended to help him deal with his condition. He'd briefly tried grief counseling after Mitchell died and wasn't keen to repeat a similar process.

There's nothing anyone can say that will make this any easier.

Naturally, his family and close friends were devastated when he revealed the awful news to them, but thankfully there hadn't been too many pitying glances – not to his face, at any rate. His in-laws took it especially hard, as they undoubtedly felt like they were losing another son. Perhaps the worst was the reaction of his nephew, who clung to Levi openly weeping in a long hug that Levi thought might squeeze the life out of him before the cancer could.

"Uncle Levi, I'm so sorry," wailed Patrick. "It's so fucking unfair."

"Yep, it is, buddy. It really fucking sucks. But you're going to be OK. And it means I'll get to be with your Uncle Mitchell again."

"You think so?"

"I know so."

I hope so anyway...assuming he isn't just a cruel hallucination.

There was, however, a far more difficult conversation to come. Levi gathered Corey and Nathalie together the following Sunday afternoon at the beach house

"I have a huge favor to ask of you both," stated Levi.

"Anything at all, we're here for you," promised Nathalie.

"That's good to know, because it might not be easy."

"You name it," said Corey.

Here goes.

Taking a deep breath, Levi steeled himself for their undoubtedly adverse response.

"I want you to help me die."

"What?! You can't be serious," exclaimed Nathalie. "I know you don't want the treatment and I respect your decision, but now you want to kill yourself?"

"I agree with Nathalie. Have you really thought about this?" added Corey.

"Please, I appreciate your concern but I've already had this argument with…" Levi looked over to Mitchell who was lurking by the bay window looking unhappy. "I've just decided and that's that."

"But…"

"You can't…"

"I don't want to die in pain," pleaded Levi, cutting their protests short. "My symptoms are already starting to get worse and I want to go out on my own terms. My birthday is in three months, I've thought about it and I want a huge party and then I'm going to take a little something to help me slip away. You don't need to worry about that part but I'm going to need you to help me with organizing the party. Can I rely on you both?"

"Yes, of course," cried Nathalie.

"You got it, partner," affirmed Corey, his eyes equally stained by tears.

The next few months were relatively busy as Levi set about putting his affairs in order. Due to his weakening condition, his lawyer, Maria Barnes, was kind enough to come to the house and help him redo his will. She was an intelligent woman with sharp brown eyes, cropped salt and pepper hair and an athletic build. The last version of his will was rather out-of-date and still had Mitchell as the sole beneficiary. There was also the matter of his stake in the restaurant. At first, Corey had refused to let Levi simply sign everything over to him.

"It's not right," protested Corey. "What about your family?"

"You're my family too, doofus." It made Levi smile using one of Mitchell's favorite light-hearted insults. "And my in-laws will be well provided for, so there's no need to feel guilty. Please let me do this for you. It'll make me happy to think of something I created living on with you."

"Fine, you bastard," agreed Corey, smiling in spite of his watery eyes. "But there's going to be a little shrine set up in your honor in the restaurant and there's not a damn thing you can do about it."

"I can live with that...or not." Seeing Corey's shocked face he smiled. "What? Too soon?"

"I'm going to miss you, partner."

"You, too."

They had an extremely long bear hug with neither of them wanting to let the moment end.

Finally, the fated day arrived and the beach house was full to bursting with revelers having a gay old time. Levi had decreed on the invites that anyone caught crying would be plied with alcohol until they stopped or passed out. As a result, Levi was pleased to see everyone enjoying themselves with only the occasional person ducking out of the room when their eyes threatened to become overly wet. In lieu of birthday presents – he was hardly in a position to appreciate them for long – Levi asked that donations be made to Picard Children's Hospital in his name. His popularity ensured that the hospital would receive quite a sizeable sum.

Surprisingly, despite his condition Levi didn't look too sick. Originally, he'd lost quite a bit of weight due to heavy pain medication suppressing his appetite but when he'd turned to medical marijuana to ease his suffering his hunger for food returned threefold and he easily gained it back. He'd also been sunbaking every day so his darkly golden skin had an incongruously healthy glow to it. Indeed, the only real obvious indications of his ill health were the dark circles under his eyes and a deepening of the wrinkles around them.

It was late September but the weather was still relatively balmy and the party spilled from the inside onto the large deck overlooking the ocean. The party had kicked off around lunchtime with everybody enjoying the bright sunlight and gentle breeze off of the water. Throughout the afternoon, Levi held court in a huge leather armchair full of cushions on the deck. The vertigo cause by his tumor made it difficult to stand for long periods and it was easier if people came to him.

Occasionally, he would see Mitchell moving in amongst the crowd and they'd exchange a secret smile. He wasn't scared in the slightest, knowing that it wasn't just a blackness he was going to, rather he was filled with the sadness of leaving his loved ones behind. More than a few times he came close to breaking his own no crying rule.

Not long before midnight, a huge white chocolate cheesecake aglow with the light of many candles was brought from the kitchen, as the assembled guests cheerily sang Happy

Birthday. After blowing out the candles, Levi acquiesced to the calls for a speech.

"Thank you all so much for being here. I'm really grateful, especially to those coming in from all over the country and beyond. A special shout out to Sara, Dean and Gigi for flying all the way here from New Zealand." Levi paused as the crowd cheered and clapped. "I realize that this is a bittersweet time for you all and I want you to know that I appreciate each and every one of you, for having had you in my life and knowing that you'll be there for one another when I can no longer be. It means the world to me that I got to see so many of you once more for such a kickass party. Now, remember the rule. No crying! Bottoms up!"

There were more cheers and many of the guests came up and gave Levi yet another series of hugs. As the night wore on people started to disappear in drips and drabs, all giving a very enthusiastic goodbye. More than a few sobs escaped the strict no sadness rule but Levi let it slide.

Finally, all that remained was his immediate family, Corey and Doctor Hastings. The latter had agreed to be on hand in case anything went awry with the special *medicine* that Levi had acquired through contacts he'd made at an online support group for people in similar circumstances. The medicine was blended in with a mango smoothie and its effects wouldn't take long to take hold.

Further down to beach, Levi had instructed them to set up a padded sun lounge with cushions all around so that he could fall asleep close to the water, listening to the waves crashing on the shore. With his nearest and dearest gathered around him, Levi gave them his last messages.

"Corey, you better keep the Samurai in fantastic shape or I will haunt you."

"Patrick, always follow your dreams and take a chance on unlikely men. You never know where you'll find yourself."

"Nathalie, Martin, Dean, Sara, you guys are the best. I couldn't have asked for a better family. I'm just sorry that it can't have been for a longer time. And Sara I'll always be grateful for your helping me to meet the love of my life."

The sky began to turn pinkish with the arrival of the brand-new day. Satisfied that he'd finished everything, Levi drank down his special cocktail.

"Mmm…fruity."

It didn't take long for him to become drowsy but before he slipped under he turned to his family one last time.

"Thanks for everything…I love you guys…Time for a nap."

And with that he fell into a contented slumber, while the small group around him let their tears flow freely.

* * *

The next morning dawned clear and bright and Levi woke up feeling surprisingly chipper. Opening his eyes properly, it took him a few moments to realize that he wasn't where he was supposed to be.

Why the Hell am I back in my bedroom? Dammit, it didn't work!

Frustrated, he jumped out of bed and was halfway across the room before he realized that something didn't feel the same. For one thing, he felt full of energy and there was no trace of vertigo or the constant throbbing in his head that'd plagued him for months. Slowly turning around, Levi saw that he was still in bed. Well, his lifeless body was, at any rate.

Oh. I guess it did work then.

He was startled by a familiar voice behind him.

"'Bout time you got here."

Spinning around, Levi came face-to-face with his husband. "Mitchell!"

Rushing forward, Levi closed the distance between them in no time and fervently embraced his husband. In Mitchell's arms, Levi felt content and whole again for the first time since his husband had been so cruelly snatched away from him. He breathed in deeply, relishing the familiar aroma of his citrus-scented cologne.

"I can't believe I can finally touch you again," cried Levi happily.

"Me too, it feels like an eternity."

They kissed again and again, holding each other in a tight embrace. Levi was half-afraid to let go lest this the reunion turn out to be nothing but a dream. After a few minutes, he loosened his grip a little, but still kept Mitchell close.

"Where is everybody?" inquired Levi.

"The family's about the house somewhere, they're waiting on the coroner to come…it was…hard for them to be in here with you."

"I imagine. I feel awful that they're grieving but I'm also so ridiculously happy. That's weird, right?"

"No, this is an odd place to be," reassured Mitchell. "It's OK. They'll move on and we have each other. That's all we need to concern ourselves with now, my sweet."

"I guess, you're right. So...what now? Do we go on to Heaven...Hell?"

"Nothing so dramatic, Vi. We do have a few options available to us. We can stay here if you like or travel about the place...visit Europe...or anywhere your heart desires, really. We aren't fixed to any one location. I've only stayed close because I wanted to be near you. And, of course, when you're ready we can move on to the next realm. I'm happy with whatever you decide, just as long as we're together."

"Happily Ever Afterlife," mused Levi.

"You could say that," agreed Mitchell with a loving smile.

Wow, it's not what I expected at all. I've been so focused on dying that I never really thought about what to do afterwards.

"Would you mind if we stayed here for a while?" asked Levi tentatively.

"In the beach house?"

"Yeah, we never did get our second honeymoon."

"Sounds perfect to me," said Mitchell giving his husband a peck on the lips. "Hope the new tenants don't mind some spiritual awakenings."

"Actually, I left the house to Patrick, so I'm sure he'll be fine with it."

"Ah, so gay adventures all around then."

They laughed companionably together before came together in a kiss that slowly built in intensity and seemed to be heading in a very naughty direction. Suddenly, Levi broke away.

"Sorry, I really want to, but I just remembered that my dead body is on the bed over there and while I may be broadminded about a lot of things, I think that might be my limit."

"Of course," agreed Mitchell with an understanding smile. "How about some fun on the beach?"

"Lead the way."

As they walked through the house, past their grieving relatives and into the bright sunshine, Levi felt his sadness fading as he looked towards the future.

This death thing isn't so bad, after all.

RIDING RED

Charlie Redman was well and truly lost, and none too happy about it. To make matters worse, the sky was becoming progressively darker, as the storm that had been threatening to break for the last hour appeared ready to deliver on its promise. After coming to the same fork in the road for the third time, Charlie pulled over to the side and banged his hands on the steering wheel in sheer frustration. The drive down from Port Davinica had been fairly pleasant and uneventful until he'd reached the woods. Now, it seemed like he'd never find his way.

All the damn roads look the same! I used to know the way to the lake house. Why the hell can't I find it now?

The oppressive heat of the mid-July day made it difficult to concentrate and only added to Charlie's ill humor. Catching sight of his reflection in the rearview mirror he scowled in disgust; his auburn locks were matted to his head with sweat, his hazel eyes looked watery and tired, and his fair complexion was red and blotchy from the heat. Not only that, his clothes were damp with perspiration and his body odor was rapidly moving toward overripe. A pair of cobalt-blue glasses sat on the front passenger seat, having been discarded in a huff, half an hour prior, after they'd kept fogging up. The air-conditioning had stopped working a week ago – something he'd meant to fix before his trip – so the windows were all rolled down in a futile attempt to refresh the air.

I'm melting! It's like being in a fucking sauna...and not in a good way. Why did I think this was a good idea again?

Looking at the map again, Charlie couldn't work out where he was going wrong. It had been a good decade since he'd been up to his grandmother's cabin and his heat-addled brain just wasn't up to the task. Neither the sat-nav in his car, nor his phone was of any help, the storm making the signal for both patchy at best.

A sudden flash of lightning, followed shortly thereafter by a deafening clap of thunder, caused Charlie to jump in his seat and spill the can of lukewarm Coke that was sitting in the console next to him.

"Fucking fantastic," he muttered darkly.

Reaching into his glove box for something to clean up the mess, Charlie encountered all manner of junk in the way, and silently cursed himself for his lack of car hygiene.

A Chipotle wrapper? I haven't eaten there in years. Ben would have a fit if he saw it. Neat freak!

Thinking of his soon-to-be ex-husband did nothing to improve Charlie's gloomy mood. He winced as yet another flash heralded the next thunderous boom. He was no great fan of storms, especially whilst sitting in a metal box on wheels in the middle of nowhere.

Fat raindrops began to splatter on his windscreen and within a few seconds he could see nothing but a great cascade of water. Quickly winding up the windows, his frustration rising to dangerous levels, Charlie turned to his meditation training – a relatively new habit to deal with an extremely acrimonious divorce. Closing his eyes, he began breathing in and out slowly, while attempting to clear the myriad of negative thoughts swirling about his brain – no easy feat. Relaxing back fully into his seat, a sense of calm began to flow through Charlie's body, as the drumming of the rain on the car roof helped to ease his mind.

A sudden flash of white light filled the dark void behind his closed eyelids, almost blinding Charlie, coupled with a roaring thunderclap that caused the windows to vibrate. Hastily opening his eyes, he saw the burning remnants of a tree several feet away from the car. Thankfully, the heavy rain soon began to extinguish the flames.

I've got to get out of this storm!

Panicked, Charlie started the car and took off down the road at a breakneck pace. He'd only made it a few hundred feet when another flash to his left attracted his attention to a small road.

There's the damn turnoff. I was so close.

Braking rapidly, he backed up and turned down the road, relieved to be finally on the right path. Mere minutes later he rounded the bend and saw the lake house. Pulling up behind the house, he quickly grabbed the shopping bags of food he'd brought, got out and ran to the covered back porch.

I'll get the suitcases when this monsoon stops.

After an uneasy few seconds where he couldn't find the keys – he'd placed them in his front pocket so he wouldn't forget where he put them – Charlie was inside. Opening the door, a wall of slightly musty air enveloped him, but he was so glad to be inside a non-metal structure that he didn't mind.

Switching on the lights, Charlie then placed the bags on the kitchen table. Looking around, he saw that the place was just as he remembered it – neat and comfortable with a thoroughly rustic vibe. And clean, just as if somebody kept up the housekeeping.

Miss you, Grandma.

Charlie hadn't been able to bring himself to visit the cabin since her passing, even though it was now legally his. He had many happy childhood memories of summer holidays spent swimming in the lake and standing by her side learning to cook all sorts of tasty treats in the kitchen. He remembered her long grey hair tied back in its habitual braid and the way her kind hazel eyes gazed down lovingly from above. Charlie also loved to cuddle into her very grandmotherly-plump build of a nighttime, as she read to him from her extensive library.

Lost in his thoughts, Charlie was startled when another brilliant burst of light illuminated the outside to reveal a hooded figure with a bearded face staring at him through the living room window. He let out a most unmanly shriek causing the face to disappear.

Running to the front door, Charlie hastily turned the lock and flung it open to see a hulking mass of manhood standing on the front porch, dripping wet with a quizzical look upon his face.

"Who the hell are you?" demanded Charlie angrily, in an attempt to cover his fright.

"I could ask you the same thing," responded the stranger just as gruffly.

There was look of annoyance in the man's penetrating, crystal-blue eyes, but it was with tinged with a mixture of great surprise and something else that Charlie couldn't quite place.

"I'm Charlie Redman. This is my cabin and you're trespassing."

"Oh, I'm sorry." A look of understanding crossed his features. "You're Elaine's grandson. The name's Bentley."

Grrrr…another bloody Ben!

"And?" demanded Charlie impatiently.

"And I'm your neighbor across the lake," explained Bentley, his gaze positively friendly as he gestured through the rain to some lights twinkling in the distance. "I've been looking after the cabin since your grandmother died. Her lawyer knows about it. I just saw the lights come on and I wasn't expecting anyone to be here."

"It was a spur of the moment trip," replied Charlie defensively. "But I'm perfectly capable of looking after myself."

The mood on the porch was becoming decidedly more awkward by the second. Unwilling to continue the conversation further, Charlie simply stared at Bentley in an unwelcoming manner. After a few moments, his new neighbor apparently got the hint.

"Right then, I should go."

"Goodbye."

Honestly, some people! Running around scaring strangers in a storm.

Barely waiting for Bentley to leave the porch, Charlie shut the door with a resounding thud and locked it up tight again before heading to the kitchen to get something for his growling stomach. Fortunately, he had all the makings for a couple of hearty sandwiches in his bags, so he quickly went to work. After he wolfed them down, Charlie turned on the dormant water heater so he could have a refreshingly long, hot shower to wash off the trauma of the day.

Thirty minutes later, thoroughly clean and wrapped up in a fluffy blue towel, Charlie went rummaging in the pantry and soon found the necessary ingredients to whip up some piping hot chocolate, which he served himself in his grandmother's over-sized red mug.

Sitting down in the large, comfy armchair by the fireplace, Charlie sipped his hot chocolate and gazed out over the water to the other side where he could just make out the other cabin through the rain. It had been an old wreck for as long as Charlie could remember, uninhabited for decades. Now that he was clean and fed, Charlie began to regret his harsh treatment of his neighbor.

Why was I so damn rude? He was just trying to be helpful, after all. I shouldn't have taken out my frustrations on him. I'll try and make amends tomorrow. I don't need any new enemies, especially if I'm going to be up here for a while. I came here to get away from my baggage, not collect some more.

* * *

To say that the last twelve months of Charlie's life were challenging would be somewhat of an understatement. Things had started to go downhill with the death of his beloved grandmother at the start of the previous summer. Even though she was in her late nineties, it had still come as a painful blow, and loaded him with a good helping of guilt. As he'd entered into adulthood, his visits had whittled down from two or three times a year to barely one, as he'd become too busy – not that he could remember what had been so important now. While they'd remained in regular phone contact, Charlie still felt like he'd let her down. The last time he'd seen her was for Christmas at his parents' house, where Charlie had made his usual empty promise.

"We'll try and come up for a week or so in the summer, Grandma."

"That would be lovely, dearheart."

Less than a month after her passing, Charlie's marriage, which had been on shaky ground for quite a while if he was to be honest with himself, fell apart. The catalyst occurred when Charlie returned home from rehearsals early one evening and was confronted with an unexpected sight. Walking into the lounge room, Charlie encountered his husband, Ben Riverton, bare-ass naked and balls-deep inside their neighbor's extremely buff college-aged son, Jacob. They had hired Jacob to do yard work and odd jobs around the house during his summer break, although this wasn't exactly what Charlie had in mind. Admittedly, Charlie hadn't failed to notice Jacob's gym-honed body and All-American good looks but he at least had remained faithful. Neither of the pair had noticed his arrival, so Charlie watched for a minute until he decided how to handle the situation. With a calmness that surprised even himself, Charlie walked over to the mantelpiece, which was decorated with a crystal vase full of roses that he'd bought Ben for their wedding anniversary a few days beforehand. He gripped the vase in his hand, walked over to the fornicating duo and poured the water and flowers directly over them.

"What the fuck?" spluttered Ben.

Looking up to see Charlie, the pair quickly sprang apart, their expressions changing from shock to fear when they realized what had happened.

"Charlie, this is the first…" began Ben.

"Mr. Redman, I didn't…" babbled Jacob, as he tried to cover himself with a cushion.

Paying no heed to their excuses, Charlie kept his voice level and what he hoped was a stony-faced expression on his features.

"Now I've got your attention, I'm going out for an hour. When I get back, I better not find either one of you here. I hope he's paying you a good rate, Jacob."

Turning on his heel, Charlie stormed out of the house and quickly drove off. He pulled over only a few blocks away, unable to contain the tears that had been threatening to burst forth since he'd caught his philandering husband cock-handed.

Several months passed, as Charlie threw himself into his work overseeing the debut of his newest play – Jessica's Wish. Nowadays, as the playwright, he normally only acted in an advisory capacity, although he'd been much more hands-on at the start of his career, turning his hand to directing and backstage work. That being said, he wasn't shy in expressing his opinion if he wasn't happy with the direction the production was taking. In his distressed state, however, Charlie wasn't at his best artistically and ended up supporting several questionable creative choices. The result was a resounding flop – his first ever.

"I don't know about Jessica, but my wish for this piece to be over wasn't granted soon enough," growled Charlie, reading aloud from the harsh theatre review in the Davinican Daily. "And that was the kindest one!"

"I don't know why you insist on torturing yourself," remarked his best friend, Lucinda Dash. "It doesn't do you a lick of good. Besides who cares what a bunch of bitter old critics think?"

A delightful slip of a woman in her early thirties with sparkling blue eyes, a jet-black pixie cut and an array of tattoos, she was forthright in her opinions.

"Audiences care! Bookings have already come to a grinding halt. It'll be a miracle if it lasts the week."

Sadly, no such reprieve was forthcoming and the play did indeed die a quiet death the following weekend. Charlie's reputation wasn't ruined; his string of previous hits saw to that, but his ego took a thorough beating. As a result, his attempts to write a brand-new show stalled. In the months that followed, he'd started and discarded nearly a dozen plays but it appeared that inspiration had left him.

"I'm finished. I'll never write again!" exclaimed Charlie for the umpteenth time that afternoon.

He was once again in the company of Lucinda, who was doing her very best to alleviate his somewhat theatrical malaise. The generously alcoholic cocktails she was plying him with were a damn good start.

"Don't be such a drama queen. It's hardly like you're ready for the retirement village; you're only thirty-six, for goodness sake. This is just a bump, that's all. You'll write another fabulous, witty comedy that everyone will absolutely love. What you do need, however, is a good dickstart."

"Dickstart?"

"You know. A kickstart with a dick. Pound your way back to happiness."

"Amusing advice from a lesbian," retorted Charlie with a slight smile.

"What can I say? I'm a delight. You've been living like a nun since you ended things with Ben. I still think you should let me cast a little spell over him, give him a nasty rash or have his bits fall off."

"Tempting, but no," laughed Charlie.

Coming from a long line of wiccans, Lucinda often talked about her passion for potions and the benefits of using spiritual energy. While he appreciated her offer, Charlie didn't really believe in that kind of thing – not that ever he'd tell her that.

"It's time to go out and have a little fun," insisted Lucinda. "You deserve it. Why don't you come out with Tabitha and me?"

I've forgotten what fun's like.

"As a third wheel to you and your girlfriend at a lesbian bar? Methinks not." He grimaced.

"It wouldn't be like that and you know it. Anyway, we'd obviously go somewhere with lots of men for you to play with."

"I don't think I'm ready to deal with men again, even just casually."

"Fine, but why don't you get away for a while? Perhaps down to the lake house?"

"I don't know." Charlie felt the grief of his grandmother's passing making an unwelcome return. "Going down there and seeing it empty will just ram home that she's really gone."

"You need to face it eventually, but if not there, then at least somewhere away from the city. Just leave everything behind… these reviews…Ben. And a change of scenery may help recharge that great big creative brain of yours."

"OK, I'll think about it."

One advantage of his profession was that he wasn't tied down to a location; as long as he had some means of recording his writing he was fine. Charlie was still reluctant to leave, as he didn't like the idea running away from his problems.

I may be just as miserable at the cabin.

The final straw came a month later when he had a nasty surprise whilst jogging in Janeway Park. It was fairly late so there was a hardly a soul in sight, but Charlie wasn't paying attention, too busy thinking about why his newest draft wasn't working. Nearing the end of his run, Charlie was about to pass through the south gate when two skinny lads in their late teens, who'd been sitting on a nearby park bench, swiftly jumped up. Grabbing an arm each, they then dragged Charlie backwards into the bushes. He was taken so much by surprise that he didn't even have a chance to cry out before he was shoved viciously to the ground and one of the pair clamped a hand over Charlie's mouth, while the other held a pocketknife to his throat. Using their legs and free arms, the pair restrained Charlie against the rough ground. He could feel twigs and leaves digging into his back and legs, as he struggled in vain against his attackers.

What do they want? Are they going to kill me? What the fuck have I done to deserve this? I should've been paying attention. I don't want to die!

"Now, you're going to be a good little boy and give us your watch and wallet," instructed the one with the knife.

"Or your face won't be so pretty anymore," sneered the other. "Do you understand?"

Charlie nodded frantically and tried to remain calm as he felt their hands roughly stripping his platinum Omega watch – an old anniversary present from Ben – from his wrist and removing his wallet from his front pocket.

"See that wasn't so bad, was it?" remarked the one who still had a knife next to Charlie's neck.

"Why don't we have some more fun with him?" suggested the other, a disturbing wealth of malevolence in his voice. "He looks like a bit of a cocksucker to me."

Oh god, they're going to rape me!

Just then the sweeping beam of a flashlight passed through the bushes.

"What's going on in there?" came a booming, masculine voice.

His attackers fled instantly and moments later a large figure was standing over Charlie with his flashlight illuminating the scene of the crime.

"Do you need help, sir?"

It took a moment for his eyes to adjust to the light and Charlie could see that the man was a police officer.

"I've...I've been mugged," mumbled Charlie in shock.

"Don't worry, sir. You're safe now." The officer gave Charlie a cursory examination and saw that there were no visible injuries bar a few scratches. "Can you walk?"

"Yes, I think so."

The officer helped Charlie to his feet and then radioed for a patrol car to meet them at the south gate. Then Charlie was taken to the station to give his statement, not that he'd been able to give them very much to go on, given the lack of light and the speed of the attack.

"That's it, I'm out of here," scowled Charlie to himself, as he left the police station. "Fuck this city!"

And so he packed his suitcases that night and set off into the woods the following morning.

Can't be any worse than staying here.

* * *

Waking up the next morning, Charlie was immediately struck by the absence of sirens or the sounds of cacophonous construction. He'd moved into an apartment in the city just after separating from Ben, as he couldn't bear to stay in their marital home, and it had been a good deal noisier than the suburbs. The storm had petered out overnight and there was nothing but the gentle serenade of birdsong coming from the outside.

I should have come down here months ago.

The memory of how appallingly he'd treated his new neighbor hit Charlie with a renewed sense of shame. He'd taken out his fear and anger on a completely innocent man who was only being neighborly. His guilt sent him into a flurry of action. After retrieving his luggage from the car, Charlie set to work in the kitchen making an apology offering. Looking out the window as he baked, Charlie noticed that the lawn was well trimmed and the garden beds were weed-free, as well as blooming with color.

Another thing I have to thank him for.

After a short, agreeable walk around the edge of the lake, Charlie knocked on the wooden door of his neighbor's cabin, with a basket full of baked goods. As he opened the door and stepped into the morning light, Charlie saw that Bentley appeared to be in his mid-forties and was ruggedly handsome with silver streaked raven hair and strong masculine features. A rather powerful-looking frame, with a white t-shirt stretching over his arms and chest in a pleasing manner, faded blue jeans clinging to thick legs and a sizeable package in front, added to the picture of virility.

Charlie experienced an almost magnetic pull toward his hunky neighbor that also caused his cock to harden at a rapid rate.

Months of abstinence had taken their toll and he was glad to be wearing tight underwear that kept his interest from becoming too obvious.

Damn, he's hot. I should've given him a much warmer welcome! Stop it. This trip is about getting away from everything...including men.

"What can I do you for?" asked Bentley with a slightly bemused expression upon his face.

Throw me up against the wall and pound me senseless! Behave! Why is he smiling like that? Does he know what I want?

Struggling to control his libido, Charlie did his best to focus on the reason for his visit.

"I...I came over to say sorry...for my behavior last night." Charlie felt an uncomfortable prickling on the back of his neck and was reminded of when he was ten and apologizing to old Mrs. Cranston for breaking her window with his baseball. "I'm sorry that I was so rude."

"I'll live."

His eyes crinkled in a friendly manner and Charlie felt a fluttering in his heart that continued to head downstairs to his nether regions.

"The least I can do is offer you these muffins. I've been experimenting; there are butterscotch-banana, chocolate chip-pistachio and blueberry-caramel ones. My grandmother would kill me if I didn't show some decent hospitality, particularly after the way you've been looking after things. I really appreciate it."

"It was no trouble. Elaine was a great lady. I was very sorry about her passing." His sadness was clearly broadcast in his tone. "Would you like to come in for a coffee? And I definitely need help with these muffins."

Should I? It's just for coffee. He's not proposing marriage. Anyway, he's probably not even into me…not after last night.

"Sure."

Walking into the cabin, Charlie was surprised by how modern the furnishings were given the rustic exterior.

He has good taste.

"So, you live here year-round, Bentley?"

"Yeah I do and please call me Lee. I'm not a huge fan of Ben."

"Me neither." Seeing Bentley's puzzled expression he explained himself. "Sorry, it's my ex's name."

"Ah. His loss."

Is he being sarcastic? Ergggh, stop over thinking everything. I need to relax.

Following Bentley into the lounge room, Charlie took a seat on the overstuffed armchair closest to the window. His host excused himself to fetch the refreshments, leaving Charlie to look out over the lake to his own cabin. Minutes later, the distinctive smell of freshly brewed coffee wafted into the room, followed shortly afterwards by Bentley bearing a tray of cups, milk and sugar. He placed them on a beautifully handcrafted wooden coffee table, which reminded Charlie of the new bookshelves he'd discovered in his grandmother's study.

"This place looks amazing. It was always a crumbling wreck when I knew it. My grandma convinced me it was haunted. I guess she just didn't want me messing about and hurting myself." Charlie felt a sad smile gracing his lips at the memory. "I'd forgotten how beautiful it is up here."

"Yeah, I grew sick of the city. Much prefer the tranquility of the woods. I made enough money working in the financial sector so that I could retire out here. I love the isolation. Ours are the only cabins occupied at the moment, so it's like having the whole woods to yourself." Bentley broke out into a jovial laugh that made Charlie smile. "How about you? Thinking of moving up here permanently?"

"No…well, actually my life is in a bit of flux at the moment. I'm not really sure what I'm doing, to be honest. I'm way behind with my work and city life has been less than inviting of late. What do you do to keep busy down here?"

"I spent a lot of time fixing up the cabin for the first year or so, then I started doing a fair bit of woodworking… this coffee table and some other pieces about the place. I even made some bookshelves for your grandmother."

"Yeah, I thought they were in a similar style."

"After all those years in offices it feels really good to work with my hands."

I bet they'd feel good working on me. Behave.

"I imagine." Charlie did his best to keep his mind out of the gutter. "I've never really been any good at things like that."

"Elaine told me you were a writer. Plays, isn't it?"

"That's right."

"Sorry, I'm not much of a theatre man."

"Ha. Well, it can be an acquired taste. I'm kinda surprised Grandma told you about it."

"You shouldn't be, she was very proud of you."

Pushing down the urge to tear up, Charlie took a bite of a butterscotch muffin and relaxed into his chair.

"Enough about me. How about you?" inquired Charlie, not so subtly prying for personal information. "No family back in the city?"

"Ah, no. My parents died a while back and my last relationship ended just before I moved up here." A sorrowful look flitted across his features. "It turned a bit nasty so I was glad for a fresh start."

"I can *definitely* relate."

They continued to chat in a companionable fashion, sharing reminiscences of Elaine. Strangely, to Charlie at least, it felt as if they were old friends, any awkwardness borne of their first encounter long gone. Glancing up at the grandfather clock in the far-right corner, Charlie was startled to realize that he'd been there for nearly three hours.

"Sorry, I didn't mean to keep you, I'm sure I've taken up enough of your time. I should get back and try to do some writing."

"It was a pleasure. Don't get much of a chance for company these days. Good luck with your writing. And any time you feel like baking up something new, you have a willing guinea pig."

"Good to know. It's always good to have someone to experiment on."

Stop flirting! Why? It's not hurting anyone. That's not why I came up here. I know, I know.

"Thanks again for everything you've done, Lee. See you soon."

"Looking forward to it."

Walking back around the lake to his cabin, Charlie had a certain lightness to his step.

This might be a much more interesting visit than I thought.

* * *

Around a week later, Charlie was sitting in the study at a large, mahogany desk, which was situated in front of a grand window giving out to a view over the lake. Apart from the kitchen, it was the coziest room in the lake house, with the heavy-looking wooden bookshelves Bentley had made, laden with numerous volumes, lining the walls. Muttering to himself, Charlie also began to fidget in an irritated manner. In a show of great frustration, Charlie threw his glasses onto the desktop and pushed his chair back sharply.

"Fuckity, fuck, fuck, fuck!"

He'd been staring at the same blank page on his laptop screen for over an hour. Usually, whenever he got stuck like this a good long run cleared out his head and let him get back to his writing. He hadn't yet gone running in the woods, as he'd been procrastinating all week and hadn't even turned on his laptop, preferring to potter about the kitchen cooking. It was a pastime that he'd neglected over the last few years and hadn't realized how much he missed it.

Might as well get some exercise or I'll be fat as well as unable to write anything halfway decent.

Donning loose blue shorts, a white singlet, a pair of scuffed trainers and his scarlet hoodie, Charlie headed out the back door and started to slowly jog towards the lake. Breathing in deeply, Charlie savored the freshness of the air and the crisp scent of pine trees. He ran alongside the water for a few hundred feet before breaking away and following one of the tracks that ran off deeper into the woods. There were little paths running all through the area and Charlie had frequently gone on long walks with his grandmother, often stopping as she showed him all the fascinating, different types of fauna and flora about the place.

Running in the woods was more challenging than the pavement he'd been pounding back in Port Davinica and sweat soon began to flow freely, dampening his clothes as he ran. After about twenty minutes, he had the disquieting sensation of being followed. Charlie slowed down and looked around but couldn't see anything but the trees.

Probably just a woodland critter. There's nothing dangerous around here…I don't think.

Continuing on his way, he tried his best to shrug off the feeling and finish his run. A short while later, Charlie came upon a small clearing that seemed vaguely familiar, so he decided to stop for a spell and catch his breath back. Sitting down on a nearby stump, he casually scanned the glade and his head swiftly came to a jerking halt. His heartbeat, which had been gradually slowing down, suddenly sped up, as did his breathing. There on the far side of clearing, just inside the tree line, was an enormous wolf, with black and silver fur and piercing blue eyes that seemed to shine in the shadows. The wolf turned its head slightly and locked its eyes onto Charlie.

Fuck! Fuck! Fuck! Fuck! What am I going to do? Is that what was following me?

It was then his natural self-preservation instincts kicked in, forcing Charlie to jump up and run. The branches and bushes scratched at the exposed parts of his legs and arms, as he ran wildly away from the clearing. He daren't look back, certain that the beast was only a few feet behind him. His heartbeat pounded in his ears as he sprinted through the woods, in what he desperately hoped was the quickest way back to his house.

After he'd been running at full tilt for five minutes, Charlie risked a glance over his shoulder and lost his footing, catching his ankle on an uncovered tree root. Crashing into some prickly bushes off to the side of the path in a spectacular fashion, Charlie felt an impending sense of doom.

This is it. This is how I'm going to die.

When he wasn't set upon straight away, Charlie scrambled to his feet and surveyed the area. The woods were still; too still, in fact. When he'd started his run, there had been a symphony of birdsong, now there was only an eerie silence.

Guess they're as scared as I am.

Treading carefully, he made his way back to the path. Looking down he saw that his legs were scraped and he was bleeding. He then began to walk along the path and realized with a start that he'd actually ended up behind Bentley's cabin. He continued on warily regarding all around him until he reached the back porch.

Letting out a breath that he didn't realize he'd been holding, Charlie was about to knock on the back door when a sudden movement by the side of his house caught his eye. He prepared to run back off into the woods like a madman when he recognized that it was a man not a monster.

"Charlie? What's wrong?" asked Bentley, his eyes brimming with concern. "You're bleeding. What happened to you?"

"There was a wolf. He chased me…I fell… then I saw you…"

Moving forward, Charlie stumbled and was deftly caught by Bentley, who moved with unexpected grace for his size. He guided Charlie inside the house and deposited him on the large caramel-colored sofa. He disappeared and reappeared a minute later with a small white medical kit and a glass of amber liquid.

"Drink this. It'll help with the shock."

Despite his usual stubbornly independent streak, Charlie welcomed the feeling of being looked after – particularly by his handsome neighbor. As he sipped the warming liquid, Charlie let Bentley swab his legs with disinfectant and put a small bandage on the worst of the wounds. It was the first time they'd touched bare skin together and Charlie couldn't fail to notice the heat radiating off of Bentley. As Bentley's large, rough hands went about their work, Charlie sensed that magnetic attraction again. Their closeness also allowed Charlie to breathe in his first dose of his neighbor's arousing, earthy scent. That and the fact that Bentley's hands seemed to be purposefully lingering on Charlie's legs, made his manhood spring to attention, straining the fabric of his shorts. He kept his hands firmly in his lap to disguise his arousal.

I'll play doctor with him any day.

"There you are, all patched up. Does it hurt much?"

"No actually, I'm just a little sore. I feel a bit silly really, I don't even know if it was really following me or not. In fact, I'm not even sure it was a wolf, now. Surely it would've caught me if it was one?"

"It's strange. Can't say I've had any wolf problems here." There was an odd quality to Bentley's voice but Charlie couldn't pinpoint exactly what it was. "Although if you want a running partner, I'd be happy to offer my services, just to be safe."

Damn, I'd love you to service me. Stop it! Why does he get me so worked up? Maybe, if I'd sex with someone other than my hand in the last year I wouldn't be so cock hungry.

"Thanks, I might just take you up on that."

"Did you want to rest up here for a while or can I help you home?"

"It's OK, I think I can make it by myself. Thanks again for your help."

"Any time. Give me a holler if you need anything at all, Red."

Red? I guess there are worse nicknames.

"I will."

As soon as he made it home, Charlie went to his bedroom ripped down his shorts and wanked furiously, his thoughts full of Bentley doing all sorts of wicked things to his body, using and abusing him like a dirty play-toy. Barely a minute later, his cockhead flared with an explosion of thick white seed that coated his hand and slowly dripped down his fingers as he lay back on the bed recovering.

Now, if only he'd do that to me in real life.

* * *

Taking Bentley up on his offer, the pair began to run through the woods most days, egging each other on before collapsing back at one of their houses for a cold beer. As the days turned into weeks, Charlie and Bentley spent increasingly more time together, enjoying leisurely chats over coffee, as well as a good many pleasant lunches and agreeable dinners. There was just something so comfortable about his neighbor's company that filled Charlie with a sense of contentment, particularly whenever Bentley used his special nickname. Not to say they didn't have the occasional disagreement.

"I don't believe it," exclaimed Charlie. "That can't possibly be true."

"'Fraid so," confirmed Bentley. "I'm a Republican."

"What is the world coming to?" said Charlie with mock exasperation. "Best we never talk of this again."

"You know the dark side isn't so bad. I'm sure we could tempt you over."

You could tempt me into anything.

As he relaxed further into the quieter life, Charlie found the words coming easier to him and his previously blank pages were now full of a rollicking new fairytale themed play – The Evil Queen and the Precocious Princess. It was a little bit of a departure for him, but his new environment had undeniably inspired him – not the least the burly woodsman living across the water.

While nothing overtly sexual had happened between them, there was an undeniable attraction on an emotional, as well as physical, level. Charlie hadn't missed the odd look of longing in Bentley's eyes but still felt himself holding him back. Apart from the demons stemming from the divorce, Charlie didn't want to make things awkward by starting something he wasn't sure he could finish, seeing he didn't know how much longer he was going to stay. While Charlie was enjoying his time away, he missed his friends in the city, especially Lucinda. They'd been chatting via Skype but it wasn't quite the same as their boozy catch-up sessions.

Maybe city life wasn't all that bad. I can't stay here forever, can I?

Sadly, nearly two months into his stay, the tranquility of Charlie's new environment was disturbed. The arrival of an official looking envelope from his lawyer's office caused a nauseous, unsettled feeling to develop in his stomach and put him in a thoroughly beastly mood.

Later that same week, Charlie and Bentley were sitting on the front porch enjoying a mid-morning coffee with some white chocolate and pumpkin scones that Charlie had whipped up earlier.

"So, are you going to tell me what's up?" demanded Bentley unexpectedly.

"Pardon?"

"You've been moping about for days now. Something to do with your ex?"

Damn, he's sharp. No use hiding it, I suppose.

Walking inside to his desk, Charlie retrieved the envelope and plonked it down alongside the scones on the small wooden table.

"I got *this* on Monday."

"It's unopened. What is it?"

"Divorce papers," huffed Charlie, the anguish clear in his voice. "It's silly, I've been the one pushing for this to be over and now I can't even open the damn envelope to sign them. I'm pathetic!"

"I think you're a lot of things, Red, but pathetic isn't one of them," grinned Bentley. "There's no shame in having a tough time with this. You did love the guy, right? I say it'd be worrying if you weren't upset by it. You're only human, after all."

"I know, you're right. It just feels like such a failure on my part. There's nothing more to be done so I should just sign the damn things."

"I have an idea that may help."

Fuck me out of my self-pity?

"I'm all ears."

"Tomorrow, you and I are going to have a big old BBQ. I'll provide the meat and the beers, you provide the dessert and anything else you want."

"OK, sounds good but I don't understand how that helps with my problem."

"Easy, we're going to have a lovely afternoon stuffing ourselves silly with good food and booze, then I'll stand by you while you sign the papers. If you need to cry, we'll cry, if you need to laugh, we'll laugh. This is a beginning for you and it should be celebrated as such."

Wow. He really is something special.

"That actually sounds kinda perfect," said Charlie, trying his best to keep his eyes from welling up in gratitude. "I'm in."

"Good to hear."

In a remarkably better mood, Charlie went about the rest of his day feeling much lighter.

I'm so lucky to have found such a wonderful neighbor...friend... something more?

Around one the next afternoon, Charlie walked over to Bentley's cabin, carrying a basket laden with goodies. The sizzling heat of the day beat down from above and Charlie was glad to be wearing a loose singlet and light, linen shorts. As he approached he could smell the mouthwatering aroma of food cooking on the BBQ, walking around the side of the cabin he could see the handcrafted wooden table laid out with food but no sign of his neighbor. Setting the basket down on the large picnic table, Charlie was about to look for Bentley in the house.

"Howdy, Red," came a disembodied voice.

"Lee?"

Looking around, his eye was caught by a slight splashing in the lake. There was Bentley waving from a way off the shore.

"It was so hot cooking, I just needed to cool off."

"Sounds like a good idea, I'll probably have a dip later too."

"I'll be right out."

With a few quick strokes, Bentley made his way to the shallower water and began to stand up. His tanned body glistened in the sunlight as the water drew away to reveal a truly spectacular specimen of manhood. His pumped-up chest was covered in a layer of curly black hair, from which his chocolate-brown, dime-sized nipples poked out. The hair then thinned out to a light dusting over his ripped abdominal muscles. As he climbed out, Charlie watched as his body tapered down in a v shape to his slim hips and he suddenly realized that Bentley wasn't wearing any swimmers.

Don't stare. Don't stare. Don't stare.

This turned out to be a nigh on impossible task as Bentley's plump manhood – at least seven inches in rest – and low hanging balls were revealed. Charlie felt his underwear becoming uncomfortably tight as he body reacted to the scene before him.

"Did you bring them?" asked Bentley, dripping wet and naked.

"Huh?"

"The divorce papers?"

Recovering the power of speech, Charlie replied in the affirmative.

"Oh, yeah. I did."

"Good man."

"I put your meat on first. You like well done, right?"

"Extremely, thanks. Can't stand to see any blood."

"Not me," countered Bentley. "I love it nearly raw."

I'd love you raw. Stop it.

Without drying himself off, Bentley grabbed a pair of faded denim cutoffs from the seat of the bench and slipped them on before walking over to the grill to check on the meat. Charlie was salivating but it had nothing to do with the aroma from the BBQ.

"Grab a beer from the cooler if you want."

"Will do."

Taking a cold bottle, Charlie sat down and tried very hard to turn his mind away from the image of perfection that was now emblazoned into his brain.

I know what I'll be wanking about later. Stop it! I need to lose my current erection first. Talk about anything else.

"It all smells so good," exclaimed Charlie, a tad overenthusiastically.

"Hope you're hungry. It's nearly done."

A few minutes later, Bentley returned to the table with a metal tray piled high with steaks, sausages and grilled vegetables.

"What do we have here?" inquired Bentley, seeing the food in Charlie's basket. "Lots of fattening goodies, I trust."

"Wasabi cheesecake, praline muffins and my own special hot sauce for the meat."

"I look forward to trying your sauce," remarked Bentley with a cheeky air.

In between much munching and drinking, the conversation flowed freely and Charlie's libido returned to a more manageable level. His head was pleasantly fuzzy after his third beer and his stomach full of perfectly cooked meat.

"What do you say we rip open the envelope and you sign these papers before we have dessert," suggested Bentley, a wide smile on his lips.

I'd do anything he asked.

"Why the hell not?"

Grabbing the dreaded envelope and a pen from the bottom of the basket, Charlie extricated the papers and placed them on the table. His hand hovered for a few seconds before he quickly signed in all the necessary spots and slammed the pen down.

I can't believe it's over. I feel…I don't know what I feel. Shouldn't I be dancing for joy? Or crying? Or something? What if it's made me emotionally dead inside?

"So, you're officially single," remarked Bentley, breaking Charlie from his reverie.

"Yeah, I guess I am."

Without thinking, Charlie gave into his baser instincts and moved forward to give Bentley a peck on the lips.

"Oh, I'm sorry, I shouldn't have done…"

Bentley didn't let him finish, returning the kiss with one of greater intensity. His beard tickled nicely against Charlie's face and he felt large arms encircling him and holding him in tight.

"I've been wanting to do that since I met you," explained Bentley with a grin. "Now, I think it's time I tried your other special sauce."

Without further ado, he pushed Charlie back against the table and kissed him hard again, while his fingers nimbly unzipped the fly of Charlie's shorts and shoved them and his red underwear roughly downward around his ankles. Once the erection had been freed, Bentley dropped to his knees and took the throbbing seven inches in his right hand and directed it towards his open mouth.

Sighing as the tongue licked over his engorged cockhead, Charlie gripped his neighbor's broad, bronzed shoulders. As more of his manhood disappeared into the warmth of Bentley's mouth, Charlie groaned louder, well aware that there was no one but the local wildlife to hear his cries of pleasure. Soon, Bentley was bobbing up and down on the cock like an expert cocksman, his right hand having moved down to take the heavy balls in hand and massaging them gently as he went about his manly toil.

Without pausing in his pleasuring of Charlie, Bentley reached around to grab the bottle of olive oil from the tabletop and coated his fingers before he began to push them against Charlie's rosebud.

Charlie gasped as the two digits breached his entrance and worked their way inside before grazing over his prostate. That proved to be more stimulation than he could take and barely thirty seconds later, Charlie's fingernails dug into Bentley's shoulders as his body began to shudder in orgasm. Crying out, Charlie jerked between the table and Bentley, as his balls unleashed their load directly down his neighbor's throat.

Not a single drop was spilled, as Bentley sucked Charlie dry before standing back up and giving him a salty kiss.

"Mmm…just as delicious as I thought it'd be," declared Bentley, his hand lightly stroking Charlie's face.

"That was…amazing!"

"I'm nowhere near finished with you yet," warned Bentley, an impish look in his eyes. "How about that swim?"

Bentley dropped his shorts again and Charlie quickly followed suit, throwing off his singlet and shaking his legs free of his shorts and underwear. Bentley took Charlie by the hand and led him into the water, where they played for a while, splashing about and trying to grab a hold of each other's slippery bodies, before coming together to kiss again, and again and again. Even in the coldness of the lake, Charlie could feel the heat radiating off of Bentley's skin.

"How do you always feel so warm?"

"Family trait," stated Bentley, with a sly smile. "Does it bother you?"

"Not in the slightest."

As they continued kissing, Bentley ran his strong hands underneath Charlie's thighs and pulled the legs up to wrap around his waist. In this position, Charlie's rosebud was exposed and it wasn't long before he felt the bulbous head of Bentley's manhood knocking repeatedly up against his entrance. Each time it prodded into him, Charlie contracted his hole, momentarily trapping the cockhead there before releasing it.

"Let's take this inside where we can do things properly," suggested Bentley.

"Lead the way, neighbor."

They exited the water, ignoring the remains of their BBQ as they walked into the house. Bentley guided Charlie to his bedroom, which had a large picture window overlooking the lake. In the middle of the room, there was a rosewood, king-sized, four-poster, bed.

"Did you make this too?" asked Charlie in an admiring tone.

"Yup," answered Bentley proudly. "Let me show you how solid it is."

Flinging Charlie to the bed in an arousing show of strength, Bentley jumped on top of him and covered his body in a series of frantic kisses. As much as he wanted to be ridden hard by Bentley, Charlie had a hunger he needed to satisfy first.

Slipping out from under Bentley, Charlie moved downward until he came face-to-crotch with nine inches of solid manhood. There was a thick vein running up its left side and a veritable stream of precum leaking from the slit on the arrow-shaped head.

Grabbing a hold of the member, it felt hot and hard in his hand. He pulled forward so that he could nibble on the thick foreskin that now covered the end. It tasted salty-sweet and he soon poked his tongue inside to lick up every trace of the delicious nectar before attempting to devour the entire thing. Gagging in his eagerness to deepthroat the magnificent monster, Charlie soon overcame his lack of recent practice and had his nose buried in Bentley's fragrant bushy crotch. From the excited noises being made above him, Charlie gathered he was doing a good job. He began to corkscrew up and down the substantial shaft, his tongue swirling around its length.

After a few minutes, Charlie could feel Bentley's body tensing up and guessed that a release was imminent. He began to work the shaft faster, desperate to taste the full load.

"Not just yet, you don't," stated Bentley pulling Charlie off of his cock.

Roughly rolling Charlie onto his back, Bentley spread Charlie's legs wide and shoved his face inside the now exposed entrance. His tongue felt divine as it eased the hole open and wiggled inside, causing Charlie to squirm in delight. The skilled rimming continued on for a good ten minutes or so, until Charlie couldn't stand it any more.

"I need you in me!" growled Charlie impatiently.

"As you wish, Red," murmured Bentley, the lust clear in his eyes.

He swiftly retrieved the necessary supplies from his bedside drawers and was promptly suited up and lubricated.

"It's been a while," cautioned Charlie.

"Don't worry, I'll be gentle," reassured Bentley, as he pushed his way inside slowly.

As the cockhead entered his sphincter, Charlie tensed up but then forced himself to relax, arching his back as he was penetrated. True to his word, Bentley took his time, gently kissing Charlie on the face and neck as he worked his member into Charlie's inner depths. It was something of an adjustment as Bentley was thicker, and a good two inches longer, than Charlie's ex-husband and it had been over a year since he'd even had that up there – in fact he was practically virginal again.

Sweat dripped onto Charlie, as Bentley toiled away between his outstretched legs. He was in absolute ecstasy, as Bentley proceeded to long-dick him for nearly an hour – his neighbor's self-control was impressive to say the least. There was an intenseness to Bentley's gaze that excited Charlie even more and gave him the definite impression that this was unlikely to be a one-time occurrence.

At last, Bentley increased his pace, thrusting into Charlie, penetrating deep inside. Their grunts and groans filled the cabin and floated outside. It wasn't too much longer before Charlie felt the load in his aching balls prepare for liberation. Bentley leaned down and latched onto Charlie's right nipple, biting down and sending a pleasurable pain shooting across his chest.

In response, Charlie's body stiffened and his cock throbbed before shooting white cream all over his heaving chest. Instinctually, his ass clamped down tight on the manhood still pounding into him, which in turn took Bentley to his well-earned climax.

Pulling out, Bentley collapsed on the bed beside Charlie and began to kiss him tenderly, while gently running his fingers along Charlie's sticky skin.

After they'd rested for a few minutes, caressing and holding one another, Bentley left Charlie's side. Positioning himself on his hands and knees, he wiggled his ass in a thoroughly suggestive manner. His cheeks spread slightly, exposing his hairy hole.

Charlie's manhood re-hardened at a rapid rate and his mouth watered. Not needing any more invitation, Charlie moved forward and dived face first into the hairy crevice and inhaled deeply. It was pleasantly musky and a little salty with the sweat of Bentley's exertion. Encouraged by Bentley's moans, Charlie used his hands to spread the cheeks even wider to taste the tangy depths of his neighbor.

"Are you going to put that lovely piece of meat inside me?" demanded Bentley, after several minutes of Charlie's enthusiastic rimming. "Suit up, soldier."

Obeying quickly, Charlie grabbed a protective sheath from the pile, rolled it on and was soon sliding himself into Bentley's searing hot passage.

Damn that feels amazing! Every part of him is hot.

He didn't have the self-control of Bentley and after hardly a minute of gentle probing, Charlie began to jackrabbit inside him. Pounding away with gay abandon, Charlie came to a rousing finish scarcely five minutes later.

Exhausted, they fell back onto the bed, panting and satisfied.

"Time to replenish our energy, methinks."

Leaping out of bed, Bentley disappeared out the door. Charlie smiled to himself as he relished the feeling of being so wonderfully used and abused. A few minutes later Bentley returned carrying Charlie's basket.

"We never did get 'round to dessert," smirked Bentley.

Liberating the cheesecake and muffins from the basket, the duo hungrily dug into the baked goods.

"Tastes almost as good as you," remarked Bentley, after finishing a large slice of cheesecake. "Almost."

Once they'd eaten their fill, they resumed their gentle affection, which unsurprisingly led to more intense play – biting, scratching and fucking hard. As they whiled away the hours, the increasingly strong, and unmistakable, musk of masculine sexual exertion perfumed the air and a growing pile of condoms filled the bin.

Eventually, after he'd lost count of his ejaculations, fatigue set in and Charlie began to drift off to sleep whilst being cuddled by Bentley from behind.

This is exactly what I needed. Hope this is just the beginning.

* * *

The next morning, Charlie awoke to find himself wrapped up in Bentley's warm and reassuring embrace, with a sizeable morning wood pressed into his buttocks from behind. His nostrils were filled with the natural woody musk of his neighbor, which combined in with the traces of their spent seed lingering on the sheets and their skin. It was the happiest and most relaxed he'd felt in months. If there weren't a pressing need in his bladder, Charlie would've happily stayed there all day.

Gingerly extracting himself from the muscular arms, so as to not wake his slumbering companion, Charlie then made his way to bathroom to relieve himself. As he was washing his hands he noticed that his back felt rather tender. Turning to examine himself in the bathroom mirror, Charlie was a little shocked to see a mess of red lines, where he'd been scratched from his shoulders all the way down to his ass.

Fucking hell! At least, it felt good getting them though.

Walking back into the room, Charlie was hit again by the heady fragrance of their play, causing his cock to stir. As he wandered back to the bed, he noticed a monogrammed silk handkerchief sitting on the corner of the wooden dresser with the initials 'BBW'. He picked it up and rubbed his fingers along the delicate material. It seemed slightly incongruous with the image of the Bentley he knew.

From his banking days, I guess.

Climbing back into bed he tried to insert himself back into Bentley's arms without waking him but wasn't particularly successful. Within seconds, the grip tightened on him and Charlie felt a bearded mouth start to nuzzle at his neck.

"Sorry, didn't mean to wake you."

"Best way to start the day, if you ask me."

They continued canoodling for a few minutes, happily rubbing up against one another, their manhoods both ready and eager for action. Curiosity suddenly gripped Charlie and he just had to know.

Brandishing the handkerchief, Charlie asked, "What do the initials stand for?"

"Big Bad Wolf," growled Bentley with a wicked grin.

"Very amusing. Well you are *big* and most definitely *bad*. But, seriously?"

"It was part of a present from my parents when I got my MBA from Harvard, monogrammed handkerchiefs, leather briefcase..." He trailed off, his eyes shiny with sadness.

"I'm sorry, I didn't..."

"No, it's fine. That was a long time ago." His familiar friendly smile resumed its place. "Anyway, in answer to your question, they stand for Bentley Byron Wilkes."

"That's a mouthful."

"So is this," added Bentley cheekily, grabbing a hold of Charlie's plump manhood before disappearing under the covers to swallow it whole.

"Oh, what a big mouth you have Mr. Wolf."

"All the better to eat you with, my dear," quipped Bentley when he resurfaced. "Any more questions?"

"Would you like to fuck me senseless again?"

By way of an answer, Bentley merely slipped his finger into Charlie's still slick entrance and pushed his way in, eliciting a gasp and a moan. From here it wasn't long before Bentley was once more balls-deep inside Charlie pumping away to their mutual enjoyment and a good deal of groaning.

Damn, I could definitely get used to this.

* * *

Several days later, Charlie drifted into consciousness to one of his favorite aromas – freshly brewed coffee. Turning over, Charlie saw that he was alone in bed. Ever since the BBQ, he and Bentley hadn't spent a night apart, alternating between their cabins. At times, Charlie felt that perhaps things were progressing a little too quickly, but as soon as they'd get naked his concerns simply disappeared in a whirl of kissing, grunting, pounding and orgasmic release.

Wrapping himself up in his faded blue bathrobe, Charlie padded out to the kitchen and was surprised to see it empty, without even a hint of percolating coffee. Confused, he made his way to his front window and looked out in time to see Bentley step off his own front porch, coffee pot in hand, apparently on his way back to Charlie's cabin. Bentley waved to which Charlie automatically responded.

Surely, I can't smell the coffee from here. That's not possible.

"Great, now I'm hallucinating," grumbled Charlie, before heading off to the bathroom for a piping hot shower to freshen up before Bentley arrived.

By the time he remerged, Charlie could hear frying sounds coming from the kitchen, accompanied by the strong scent of bacon, eggs and toast.

"Hey Sleepy-red. You were out of coffee, so I made some at mine and brought it back. I've already poured you a cup."

"You're an angel," exclaimed Charlie, giving Bentley a peck on the cheek before sitting down with his cup of liquid energy.

"Mmm…it's so good, I could swear I could smell it from across the lake."

Instead of laughing like Charlie thought he would, Bentley just gave him a small, funny smile. They finished their breakfast in a companionable manner before parting ways, Bentley to do some maintenance on his cabin and Charlie to work on his play.

A week later, Charlie was tidying his bedroom when he knocked a book off the top of the bedside table. Bending down to retrieve it, he discovered that his glasses were resting just under the bed frame with a layer of dust gathering on them.

"Must have dropped them," muttered Charlie.

As he was wiping them clean, Charlie realized he couldn't remember the last time he actually put his glasses on. His vision wasn't so bad that he needed to wear them constantly but he tended to get mild headaches if he didn't wear them for long stretches in front of the computer. Given how much he'd been writing of late, he should've noticed their absence well before now.

Could my eyes have gotten better? Maybe it's the clean country living?

Shrugging, Charlie placed the glasses on his bedside table and kept tidying up, barely giving the matter another thought.

Another week passed and Charlie caught himself humming in the kitchen as he prepared a romantic dinner for himself and Bentley. As much as he didn't want to admit it, he was very much under Bentley's spell. Their passionate play had only increased in ardor and Charlie often found himself staring out the window at Bentley's cabin like a love-struck schoolboy. The prospect of a future with Bentley appeared infinitely more inviting than the thought of returning to live in the city.

As Charlie opened a packet of raw mincemeat that he'd been planning to turn into spaghetti bolognaise for dinner, he was struck by a peculiar craving. Looking at the uncooked meat, Charlie began to salivate. He tentatively put his fingers down to grab a small piece. Bringing it to his mouth he was filled with an intense hunger. He quickly devoured the piece in his hand and before he half-realized it, Charlie had finished all the meat and was licking the plastic tray it'd been sitting on.

What the fuck is wrong with me? Is that even sanitary? Have I turned into a rabid animal? I guess people do eat things raw sometimes. Still, it's odd. Looks like I'll be making a vegetarian sauce instead.

He finished up and then bustled about setting the table, putting a candle in the middle for ambiance. Retiring to the bathroom, Charlie fussed about in front of the mirror getting ready for his guest to arrive.

"I know that this is going to sound bizarre but I've felt *different* lately," mentioned Charlie, as he sat eating dinner across from Bentley. "I don't know whether it's all the fresh air or being close to nature or the lack of city noise but my senses really seem to be ramped up. Almost like I'm superhuman...or maybe pregnant."

Bentley laughed at the joke but Charlie thought it seems half-hearted at best.

"Something wrong?" asked Charlie worriedly. "You think I'm a nutter, don't you?"

"No, not at all," reassured Bentley, although he had a peculiar look in his eyes. "Tell me, have you...started craving raw meat?"

Did he see me? Why didn't he say anything?

"Yes! How did you know? It was the weirdest thing. Is this some sort of side effect of living in the woods?"

"Sort of. I...umm...I...I have a confession to make as well."

Uh oh. I knew he was too good to be true. Calm down, it's probably nothing serious.

"You're married with a wife and kids tucked away in the city?" teased Charlie, in an effort to ease his own concerns with humor. "I knew it! Can't trust you wood folk."

"Ah, no. It'd be easier if it were something that simple. What's happening to you is...is because of me."

"What do you mean?"

"The reason that you've been feeling different is because we're having sex."

Is he serious? I sure know how to pick them.

"Umm, sounds like someone's a little conceited. Don't get me wrong, it's been pretty damn awesome but..."

"I'm a werewolf."

No, I definitely didn't hear that right.

"Excuse me?"

"I'm a werewolf and because we've been having so much sex, some of my *attributes* have transferred to you though the scratches and the exchange of our...bodily fluids."

Oh, come on. That's just ridiculous. Ohhh, I get it!

"How romantic," laughed Charlie. "I thought you were serious there for a sec. You have a great poker face."

"Shall I prove it to you?" offered Bentley solemnly.

"Sure go ahead."

I've been sleeping with a crazy man. No wonder the sex was so hot.

Looking at Bentley, his amusement soon faded and Charlie got a sinking feeling in the pit of his stomach. Right before his eyes, Bentley's whole face became narrower and his ears grew more pointed. His beard appeared to thicken and started to cover his face.

"WHAT THE FUCK?!"

Leaping up from his chair, Charlie rapidly backed away. In his haste he tripped over the corner of the coffee table and ended up sprawled on the floor. Scrambling to his feet, Charlie ran for the front door and frantically tried to turn the lock.

"Red, wait!" called Bentley, his face resuming its human form. "Please, I'm not going to hurt you."

"Get away from me! You're a monster!" screamed Charlie, his fingers trembling too much to be of use on the door.

"Charlie, please calm down it's still me. I'm still the same guy, I just turn into a wolf sometimes."

The lock clicked open and Charlie yanked open the door. He was about to run for his life when he registered what Bentley had said and he was hit with a sudden revelation. His fear took a backseat to anger as he whirled around to confront his shape-shifting neighbor.

"It was you!" shouted Charlie. "The wolf in the woods that day."

"Yes," admitted Bentley reluctantly. "But I didn't chase you. You ran as soon as I turned my head. I never meant to frighten you or for you to get hurt. I'm truly sorry about it."

"You lied to me! You said there was no wolf problem here."

"Technically, it isn't a problem," justified Bentley with a weak smile.

"Don't try and get cute with me."

"Can we please just sit down and talk about this?" pleaded Bentley. "I promise I'd never hurt you."

Curiosity caused Charlie's anger to fade slightly and he walked back towards the table at a slow measured pace that belied his inner turmoil.

"OK. You have five minutes," instructed Charlie, as he sat back down. "And then I want you out of my house."

"That's fair," agreed Bentley also resuming his place at the table. "My...*condition* runs in my family. My father was one, as was my grandfather and so on."

This can't be happening. I don't like having to shave as is.

"So am *I* a werewolf now?"

"No...not yet. The changes you've been experiencing will start fading as soon as we stop sleeping together. In about a week or so you'd be back to normal."

"Oh."

The thought of no longer sharing a bed with Bentley bothered Charlie a good deal – knowing he'd miss the intimacy as well as the sex. The idea of losing his superior senses was similarly unappealing.

"Unless you didn't want to be *normal*," added Bentley, apparently picking up on Charlie's disappointment.

"What are you saying?"

"If you wanted, I could make you like me. But there is more to it than just your improved senses and desire for raw meat. You wouldn't get sick any more, as we're immune from disease and we do tend to live slighter longer than normal people. That being said, the change from man to wolf is extremely painful and to start with you won't have any control over the beast within. It takes a lot of training but with practice you'll eventually have full command over the supernatural side of you."

This is all too much!

"I...I'm still trying to process that this is really happening." A new idea suddenly occurred to Charlie. "If werewolves are real, does that mean that all monsters are?"

A look of great annoyance tinged with hurt passed over Bentley's handsome features.

"I'm not a monster! I can't help the way I was born and I've never hurt anyone intentionally." Softening his tone, Bentley continued. "But yes, most supernatural creatures in books and films have a basis in reality."

"So, vampires and spirits?"

"Yup. Fairies and guardian angels too."

"Goddamn! I just...I...this is all..." Charlie struggled to process all this fantastical new information. "What now?

"I know it's a lot, but please think about my offer. I knew as soon as I saw you that we were meant to be together. If you joined me, we could have such an amazing life. I love you, Red. Don't tell me that you don't feel the same connection."

I do feel it. But to become a werewolf?

"Honestly, I do care about you, but I don't know if I'm ready to take such a big step...or even if I'll ever be ready. You know I have trust issues after what happened with Ben and I can't just jump headlong into another commitment with a man who hid things from me. I need time to think."

"I understand and I'm truly sorry. I should have told you before we became involved but there's nothing I can do about that now. It's a lot to process so please take as long as you need. I'll keep my distance until you're ready to talk about it." Bentley got up to go but paused by Charlie's chair. "If it helps any, wolves mate for life."

Then he was gone, leaving a very bewildered Charlie in his wake. Remaining at the table, Charlie was lost in a whirlwind of thoughts.

A werewolf! My life certainly isn't boring. Can I trust him? How can this be real? Mating for life doesn't sound so bad though. Is that what I want?

*   *   *

A week passed without Charlie speaking to Bentley, although he had seen him working in his yard and around the cabin. As Bentley had explained, Charlie noticed his cravings and senses dampening back down to normal, although he missed them terribly.

It was really like being a superhero.

Since their dinner, he'd thought of pretty much nothing but Bentley's proposal and was still no closer to a decision. To help him with his conundrum, Charlie invited Lucinda up to the cabin for the weekend – she'd jumped at the chance as her girlfriend was away on family business. He hadn't told her, or anyone for that matter, about Bentley, as at the time he hadn't wanted to jinx the burgeoning relationship. Given her Wiccan heritage, Charlie imagined that Lucinda would at least be open to the conversation, without thinking him a total lunatic.

Charlie had just finished lunch when he heard the familiar sound of Lucinda's jeep pulling up behind the house. Dumping his plate in the sink, he went to open the door before she even had a chance to knock.

"Charlie!" squealed Lucinda, before diving forward for a big warm hug. "It's been *forever*! You sounded so mysterious on the phone. What's going on? You've met a guy! I can tell. I told you it was the best thing to get out of the city. So, tell me everything!"

"I think first we need a drink."

After retrieving her belongings from the jeep, Charlie shepherded her inside and went to pour them both two very large gin and tonics – their preferred drink for heavy discussions. Once they were settled on the sofa, Charlie told her the entire story from meeting Bentley, to seeing the wolf, his temporary abilities and finally Bentley's confession and proposal.

"What do you think?" asked Charlie cautiously.

"Wow!" exclaimed Lucinda. "You're so lucky!"

"So, you believe me?"

"Of course, I do, although I've known about the existence of supernatural species for a while now." There was a touch of smugness to her tone. "I'm even friends with a vampire, he's one of the nice ones though. But to have a chance to become one is so amazing. You do want to do it, don't you?"

"That's the thing; I don't know. It was strange having those new skills and things were going great with Lee until I found out the truth. I'm not sure if I'm ready for that kind of commitment. I've only just gotten divorced and I haven't really known him all that long. Isn't it all a bit soon? Although the sex is the best I've ever had."

"Forget about your head and your dick, what does your heart say?"

"Listening to my heart is how I ended up married to Ben."

"From the sounds of it Lee is nothing like Ben, especially if he's talking about mating for life. But you're the one who has to make the decision. Whatever you choose you have my total and utter support, although it would be infinitely cool to have a werewolf for a best friend."

"Well, then. That's the only reason I need," teased Charlie, poking out his tongue.

"Good boy. Now, tell me how your latest opus is going."

The rest of the weekend passed by in an agreeable blur of gossip and laughter – and the occasional spying on Bentley from a distance. Sadly, all too soon it came time to say goodbye.

"Thanks for a lovely country escape and remember to follow your heart, my lovely," counseled Lucinda.

"Say hi to Tabitha for me."

After he packed Lucinda back into her jeep, Charlie watched her drive off and then stood there for a few minutes, deep in thought. Abruptly coming to a decision, he set off at a brisk pace. Instead of returning inside, he walked around the house and towards the lake and then kept going until he was standing on Bentley's porch, hammering on his front door.

An uncertain-looking Bentley soon opened the door.

"Yes!" Charlie proclaimed with determination.

"Yes?" questioned Bentley. "You mean you…"

"I love you, too and I want you to do it. Make me like you. Scratch me, bite me, do whatever you have to do. Make me a werewolf, now!"

Before I chicken out.

"It doesn't work quite like that. We actually need to wait for a full moon. And it does involve a bite and taking my seed but…"

"Great. Best we start practicing now then."

Pushing Bentley backwards into the cabin, Charlie took total control, not that his neighbor objected in the slightest. Minutes later, they were naked and rolling around on the bed together, making up for over a week's deprivation from one another.

Much later that night when they had exhausted their balls, the pair was cuddling and Charlie felt happier than he had in a long time.

"When is the next full moon, then?" inquired Charlie.

"At the end of next week, but we should probably wait until the one after," advised Bentley.

"Why?"

"Because it's a Blood Moon, which is sacred to our people. To transform during one gives you an amazing high. It also falls on Halloween, which is a time of heightened supernatural power."

"I thought that was just a myth."

"What can I say? Sometimes stereotypes are right. Trust me, it'll be worth the wait. Besides, I'm pretty sure I can keep you distracted until then."

To prove his point, he moved down Charlie's body and commenced an attack on the already well-abused crotch. Charlie gasped and grunted at the expert mouthwork, grasping at Bentley's head and shoulders.

I guess it won't be so bad to wait.

* * *

Notwithstanding Bentley's frequent distractions, the wait felt interminable. On the plus side his senses had returned to their previously heightened levels, which delighted Charlie to no end. Ever since Charlie had agreed to be turned, the pair had spent every night together. They'd long abandoned condoms as Bentley's state meant they weren't necessary, so their sex had become even more raw and intense.

Almost as excited by the upcoming transformation was Lucinda, who'd been positively thrilled when Charlie told her of his decision.

"It's going to be so awesome!" squealed Lucinda. "I can't wait to see you go full wolfman!"

"I don't know about that, it'll take a while to get used to but maybe at some point."

"You better call me when it's all done."

"Promise."

At last the fated day arrived and Charlie felt like a little boy waiting for Christmas morning, an odd sensation seeing it was only Halloween.

As the sun came to set, Bentley appeared at the door.

"Follow me," he commanded.

Hand in hand, they walked together in silence at a leisurely pace. The eclipse wasn't due to start for over an hour so they weren't in a rush. Despite it being the end of October, the weather was still unseasonably warm, and a gentle breeze rustled the leaves about them. They soon broke free of the woods and stepped into the clearing where he'd first seen Bentley in wolf form.

"We don't want to be inside for the first change," Bentley had advised Charlie.

As they walked to the center of the glade, Charlie looked up to see the full moon high in the sky. A storm was brewing and heavy clouds began to blot out the stars.

"Time to strip down," instructed Bentley, in his deep baritone.

Shivering from excitement, Charlie's fingers trembled as he tried to undo the button fly of his jeans.

"Let me," offered Bentley.

They then helped each other undress until they were both standing naked in the field.

"So...do we have to wait till the eclipse?" asked Charlie, his need evident.

"Not at all."

Moving forward, Bentley took Charlie into his arms and looked lovingly into his eyes.

"This is the last chance to back out. I'll completely understand...well, maybe not completely."

"You aren't getting rid of me that easily," retorted Charlie, as he pulled Bentley even tighter to him.

They soon became lost in a series of frantic kisses as the light breeze around them picked up pace, shaking the leaves in an increasingly agitated manner. They rolled around naked on the ground, the foliage crunching underneath them. A flash of lighting lit the entire field and was followed ten seconds later by a peal of thunder. At any other time being out naked in a field during a storm would have been terrifying to Charlie but he had never been so aroused in his life.

The air felt full of electricity and Charlie saw from the corner of his eye that the moon had begun to take on a reddish tinge. Looking back to Bentley he saw that his boyfriend's eyes had become brighter and were practically glowing in the darker light. Another flash of lighting seared the sky and Bentley growled.

"It's time."

Rolling Charlie on his back, Bentley spat on the entryway for lubrication before he speared his cock inside Charlie's passage.

Crying out in a mixture of pain and pleasure, Charlie then gritted his teeth as Bentley pounded away into his ass. Above him the sky was alive with color and movement as the clouds were flung about by the wind, interspaced with lighting and the huge increasingly red moon.

Several minutes later, the eclipse was at its peak. Bentley hammered away with such ferocity that his hips were almost a blur, battering into Charlie who'd never been so roughly taken. He thought he may pass out from the sheer intensity of it but he kept his focus on Bentley and the animalistic visage he'd taken on, looking more and more lupine by the second.

At last his strenuous efforts paid off and Bentley let out a howl as he came. Charlie felt the solid member throb and the hot seed start to spurt. It felt different to their previous times and was almost like it was burning his insides as it coursed deep within him. The heat spread through Charlie's body heating his crotch; his balls felt like they were in a sauna. Within seconds they contracted and their load exploded out in the most intense orgasm of his life. Ropes of cum sprayed upwards, splattering back down onto his chest, face and above his head.

The unnatural heat continued to flow throughout his body making it harder to concentrate on anything but being totally consumed by Bentley. Just when he thought he couldn't take anymore, Bentley moved forward with an inhuman speed and sunk his teeth into Charlie's neck causing him to cry out from the overwhelming sensations wracking his body. There was an explosion of light as multiple strikes of lighting hit the trees surrounding the clearing.

It was all too much and Charlie had the impression of falling into a dark well, the light rapidly fading around him with the sensation of Bentley's manhood still fully lodged inside. It felt as if they were no longer two separate beings but were now connected in a most primal of ways. The last things Charlie saw were Bentley's glowing blue eyes staring deep into his.

Damn, that was…weird.

* * *

The next morning, Charlie was awoken by the sounds of birds chirping loudly right next to his head. Moving his head slightly, he saw that the birds were actually in the trees at the edge of the clearing. All trace of the previous evening's storm had been erased from the skies and there was nothing but an intense blue expanse above him. The sun beat down on their exposed bodies, adding to their already elevated temperature.

His whole body felt energized, as if he'd had the best sleep ever and topped it up by mainlining some coffee. He felt strong and sharper than he ever had before. And he was ravenous…and not just for food. His morning wood felt like a steel rod and having it resting between the furry cheeks of Bentley's amazing ass only added to his appetite.

Charlie debated whether or not he should wake Bentley to get his needs met when his boyfriend began to stir of his own accord.

"Good Morning, Red," greeted Bentley with a sleepy voice.

"Good Morning to you, Mr. Wolf," replied Charlie, while nuzzling his boyfriend's neck. "Everything feels so much more intense this morning."

"It will take you some time to get used to your new body, although it feels like someone wants to be Top Dog, this morning."

"I guess were both true cockhounds now. Would you mind?"

Firmly running his hands over Bentley's chest, Charlie pulled his boyfriend even closer. He ground his hips harder against Bentley, who responded by pushing back against the eager manhood and squeezing his buttocks around it.

"What do you think? I'm ready to ride if you are!"

Using the sweat between Bentley's buttocks, from the body heat they'd been generating together, Charlie was easily able to slide his manhood down and maneuver it against the hairy entrance. Once in position he pushed gently, the thick mushroom head was supplying more than enough precum to lubricate its way inside. He felt the welcoming warmth of the moist passage as he pressed forward. Inch-by-inch, he edged his cock inside and began to make slow gentle love to his mate.

I could definitely handle this the rest of my life.

LOVE AT FIRST DEATH

Jules O'Lantern glided across the rink with the experienced ease of a long-time skater. He adored the sensation of almost floating, as it helped him clear his mind of all his day-to-day worries. This was particularly needed today after he'd spent a good chunk of the morning and early afternoon dealing with a cantankerous client, who was disputing the quality of Jules' work. This annoyed Jules to no end, as he prided himself on his attention to detail. Unfortunately, his distracted state meant that his reflexes were a tad slower than usual, so when a man unexpectedly crossed into his path they collided forcefully and crashed down to the ground in a tangled heap of limbs.

"I'm so sorry," gushed Jules apologetically. "Are you, OK?"

"It's fine," replied the stranger a tad grumpily. "Be more careful."

And with that the man got to his feet and skated off. Despite the shock and irritation of the collision, Jules hadn't failed to notice the man's liquid brown eyes, and short, dark cropped hair that accentuated his strong, swarthy, features.

Over the course of the next hour, Jules tried to stop himself from openly ogling the man, but just couldn't seem to pull his gaze away. In his defense, the way the man's jeans clung to his pert bubble butt, as he skated around the rink, was truly giddying. It was with no small delight that Jules soon discovered the attention wasn't purely one-sided. More often than not when his eyes sought out the strapping skater, there was a reciprocal look of interest on the man's handsome face.

Looking down at his watch, Jules realized that he needed to finish up if he wanted to have enough time to get home and change before his family dinner later that evening. He exited the rink and exchanged his skates back for his bright blue converses and was finishing tying up the laces when he noticed the object of his lust standing at the far end of the wooden bleachers staring at him. The man smiled at Jules and gave a tilt of his head, in an apparent indication that he wanted to be followed, before he moved out of sight behind the bleachers.

I'm going to be late. This better be worth it.

Taking the hint, Jules walked over to where the man had been standing and saw him passing through a wooden door at the end of the corridor. Following him into the dimly lit room, Jules quickly realized from the piles of broken skates and rolled up banners that it was an old storeroom. The air had a mustiness to it and it was evident that the room didn't see much use. As he moved further into the storeroom the door shut behind him with a thud. Spinning around, Jules saw the man standing there with an impish glint in his eyes.

This ought to be interesting.

"Hi," greeted Jules.

The man responded by moving forward, pushing Jules up against the wall and kissing him in a hearty fashion. Further aroused by the man's spicy-sweet scent, Jules responded in kind as their hands joined in on the fun, groping and pulling each other closer. Rapidly hardening members rubbed together through the material of their jeans, as they continued their amorous affection.

Through their fervent kissing, the lad unzipped Jules's jeans and pushed them down around his ankles. Sinking to his knees, he squeezed Jules' sizeable erection through the thin blue material of his underwear.

"Nice!" remarked the stranger.

Without further ado, he yanked down the underwear and freed the solid manhood. Taking it into his hand, the man brought the slick head to his lips and he commenced lapping up the sweet nectar that was drizzling from the eye. Jules gasped as the man then proceeded to take all of the nine inches into his throat without even a hint of a gag reflex. In his experience with men – and he'd had a lot – there'd barely been a handful of guys, who'd managed such a feat.

A true cocksmith.

Proving him correct, the man skillfully milked Jules' manhood with the suction of his mouth and swirling tongue. Cupping the large balls in his hand, the lad massaged them with a firm, even pressure.

After a few delightful minutes of fellatio, the man stood straight up into another hungry kiss with Jules. Unbuttoning the skater's jeans, Jules fully intended on reciprocating the man's efforts, but his playmate apparently had other ideas. Pushing down his own jeans the stranger turned around to reveal a fetching pair of red and black bottomless jocks, which put his pleasingly round buttocks on full display.

"Mmm...easy access," growled Jules.

"Why do you think I wear them?" he replied, giving Jules a cheeky look over his shoulder.

Not one to refuse such a tempting invitation, Jules dropped to his knees and spread the cheeks apart with his hands. He leaned forward and slowly licked around the hairless hole, savoring the sweaty musk while his hands kneaded the plump buttocks. He bathed the hole in his saliva and loosened it slightly with this tongue. The lad moaned his appreciation and tilted his hips back against Jules' face. Pushing his face in deeper, Jules chewed and sucked on the rosebud as his tongue darted in and out. It didn't take much of this eager feasting before Jules hankered for something heartier. Standing up, he pulled the man close, his manhood pressing into the crease between the cheeks, leaving a sticky smear as his cockhead touched the bare skin.

"Got protection?" asked Jules hopefully.

"Yup."

Bending down to his small leather satchel, the man quickly rifled through it and soon produced a packet and a small bottle of lube to go with it. Jules took the offered condom and hurriedly rolled it on himself. After lubricating the latex and then the tight entrance, Jules began to ease his cock inside, massaging the man's cock through the stretched and increasingly damp material of his underwear. He started off slowly, easing his cock into the extremely snug passageway, but the way his playmate pushed back told Jules that this was far from the man's first time.

As he sunk his inches inside the tunnel, it stretched to accommodate him and in turn caused a good deal of happy squirming from the stranger. Jules kept pushing until he was buried to the hilt, which elicited a loud groan of satisfaction. Starting off with small, quick thrusts, Jules then progressed to faster and deeper movements. Gripping the man's lean hips, he took great pleasure in fucking the man hard up against the wooden wall. The air in the small room quickly became heated with their play and beads of sweat formed on Jules' brow and dripped down onto the man's exposed lower back. Both men were grunting with their exertion, but the loud music playing over the sound system made it unlikely that anyone would hear their sounds of sodomy. As much as he wanted to stay and plow that ass for hours, Jules knew his time was limited. Mindful of the hour, he began to race towards his own release, as the passage contracted sensually around his member.

Pounding away like a man possessed, Jules shortly felt that familiar tingling in his balls signaling an imminent release. His breathing hitched and his body shuddered, as he ejaculated into the protective sheath. Pulling out, Jules discarded the condom, spun the man around and ripped down his underwear to free the eight uncut inches that were ready to play. He sunk to his knees again and licked off the sticky juice that coated the head and foreskin, before taking the member in his mouth and swallowing it down to the base in a practiced move that had the man gripping the back of Jules' head and holding him tight.

After the stimulation of the hurried fuck, the man was clearly ready to explode. Barely a minute of Jules' satisfying treatment was needed before the lad tensed up and shot his thick, creamy load into the waiting mouth. Jules greedily gulped it all down – it was one of his favorite beverages, after all.

Once he'd thoroughly drained the last drop of seed, Jules stood back up and gave the man a soft kiss.

"I'm Jules, by the way."

"Cain," grinned the man. "Pleased to meet you."

"You, too. Sorry, it was so fast but I gotta run."

"No problem, it got the job done." Pulling up his jeans, Cain then gave Jules a longer kiss that had his manhood rising once more. "See you 'round."

Jules didn't offer his number and neither did Cain. Evidently, both thought that the experience would be a one-time affair. They rearranged their clothing and soon went on their separate ways. On the drive back home to change, Jules noticed in the rear-view mirror that he had a dopey smile on his face.

Damn he was a hot fuck. Pity we won't get a second go around.

Little did he know that their chance encounter was going to lead to heartbreak, suffering and death.

* * *

An hour and a half later, Jules was knocking on the big wooden door of a two-storey home in the suburbs of Port Davinica, only ten minutes tardy. Seconds later, he heard the sound of many small feet racing towards the door before it was enthusiastically flung open.

"Uncles Jules!" chorused his adorable six-year-old nieces, Amy and Isabelle, as they lunged forward to engulf him in a hug.

"Let him breathe," joked his brother-in-law, Seth; a handsome man with kind hazel eyes, sandy dark-blond hair and a tanned athletic build.

"Naw, they're fine," said Jules, hugging the pair tightly back.

Once released from their death-grip, Jules walked into inside to find his brothers, Jock and Jasper, talking to one another over by the kitchen. As always, it was like looking at alternate universe versions of himself. He was one of a set of identical triplets, the three sharing the same bright green eyes, straw colored hair, a tall stature, pale flawless skin and a predilection for men. Their personal styles, however, varied markedly. While Jules favored a more athletic street-casual look with his hair worn in a long, floppy style, Jock's hair was cropped short and he preferred more formal attire, whereas Jasper projected a conservative, bookish vibe, reinforced by his blue, thickly-framed glasses.

Family time was important to the brothers and they all sat down to dinner together at least once a week. Even though the three of them ran a popular handyman service together, these days they didn't spend as much time in one another's company. For many years they had shared a house in another suburb on the far side of the city but that came to an end when Jasper married Seth a decade ago. Jules had also fled the nest a few years later to move in with his then-boyfriend, although that had ended on a rather sour note. Nursing a bruised ego and a touch of heartbreak, Jules had moved back in with Jock and the two had continued their carefree bachelor lifestyle ever since.

After exchanging greetings, they sat down to a scrumptious dinner of roast chicken and baked vegetables – courtesy of Jasper – with much chatter and laughter, before it was time for the little ones to say their goodnights.

Once the girls were put to bed, after demanding story after story from their overly indulgent uncles, the men retired to the back terrace for some dessert wine. It was a pleasant July evening and a sweet floral scent, bordering on cloying, wafted from the colorful garden beds around them – Seth had developed a rather green thumb following their move to the suburbia.

Jules had barely started sipping his wine before the interrogation began.

"Alright, spill," demanded Jock with a knowing smile.

"What about?" asked Jules, being deliberately vague.

"Please, we can all see it," added Jasper.

I hate that they can always tell. Damn telepathic link.

"Fine. There was a guy at the roller rink," admitted Jules.

"And?" insisted his brothers in unison, like eager schoolboys.

"We fucked in a storage cupboard behind the bleachers and it was pretty damn hot. And that's all you're getting out of me."

"Spoilsport," retorted Jock.

"It's hardly like you're lacking in that department," taunted Jules.

"Doesn't mean that I don't like hearing about it."

"Seeing him again?" asked Seth, his romantic side shining through.

"Doubtful."

"You know, it wouldn't kill you to date," added Jasper, who shared his husband's starry-eyed idealism when it came to matters of the heart. "I mean you haven't dated anyone since..."

"Don't you dare mention his name!" warned Jules, in a severe tone.

"Since...*you-know-who*," continued Jasper cautiously. "All you do is have random shag after shag."

"And why shouldn't he? It's fun. It's what I do and I love it!" boasted Jock.

"Well we all know that you're incapable of experiencing any feeling that doesn't involve your cock," sniped Jasper lightheartedly.

"Meh, saves all this wishy-washy heartache business."

For people who were identical on the outside, their insides couldn't have been more different. That being said, there was a time that all three of the brothers avoided becoming overly attached to the guys they played with, especially the humans. Indeed, it was something of a family tradition to stick to their own kind, namely other supernatural beings. The members of the O'Lantern family, while human in appearance, were far more than they seemed. To be exact, they came from a long line of guardian angels and were very much intertwined with the forces of life and death, with their primary role of helping lost spirits cross over to the other side. Over the years, the brothers had witnessed too many humans they cared about grow old and sick, while they lived on in perfect health. Their extremely long lifespan dwarfed that of humans, hence the rule.

That was, of course, until Jasper had met the thoroughly natural Seth and been swept off his feet. One bright side was that if they wished the brothers could transfer a part of their essence to extend the longevity of their human partner, as Jasper had done for Seth. The drawback being that it shortened their own. It was an enormous commitment and sacrifice that Jules wasn't sure he'd ever be able to make.

Maybe I haven't met the right guy. Or he just doesn't exist. Jasper found Seth. Fluke of nature. What's the chance of that happening again?

And so, for his part, Jules had only dated other supernatural creatures. The latest of these had been Harrison Fee, a striking man with blond shoulder-length locks, violet-blue eyes and a tall, lean build...and who happened to be a fairy. Their tumultuous relationship was the reason that Jules hadn't dated for the last five years.

After fending off further inquiries into his personal life, Jules and his brothers passed a pleasant time on the terrace chatting about future vacation plans and interesting projects they'd been hired for in the coming weeks. As it began to grow late, Jules made his goodbyes and jumped in his car to head home. Jock had driven there separately in their work van, as he'd had a job in the area just before the dinner. Jasper appreciated the solitude on his way home as it gave him a chance to think about things.

Are they right? Should I put myself out there again? Even if I don't go with a human, even being with another supernatural doesn't guarantee a happy ending. Maybe Jock has the right idea? Do I want to be alone forever?

* * *

Regardless of his reluctance to get involved with anyone, it seemed that the gods had other ideas. The following week, Jules proceeded to run into his recent playmate with an almost eerie regularity.

On Monday evening, Jules finished off a simple electrical job for a nice elderly couple in Graywood Gardens, a large apartment complex overlooking Janeway Park, and found himself in desperate want of a caffeine hit. Opportunely, at the base of the building there a funky-looking café called Perk Up.

Exactly what I need.

Just as Jules was entering he nearly ran into a familiar figure exiting – Cain – the man from the roller rink. The two exchanged a conspiratorial smile and Jules was tempted to say something, but the moment was lost when two teenage girls also intent on leaving interrupted them.

"Excuse me," sniped the taller of the pair, glaring at Jules disdainfully.

Shaking his head ruefully, Jules moved aside and entered the café. By the time he turned around Cain was crossing the road into the park, but Jules still appreciated the view.

On Wednesday afternoon, Jules smiled at his reflection, pleased with the result of his haircut and facial at a men's grooming salon – L'Hommerie. It was the first time he'd been there and he was using a gift voucher that Harrison had given him for his birthday a few months prior, during one of their civil periods. Even though they had a rocky history, Harrison still could be thoughtful on occasion, just not faithful. Feeling refreshed, Jules walked out the front door and narrowly missed colliding head on with someone rushing in.

"Oops, sorry," apologized Cain. "This is getting to be a habit."

"It's OK. You owed me one."

Before he could say anything else, Cain grinned and rushed inside leaving Jules standing in the doorway.

Hesitating, Jules thought about getting Cain's number but the moment didn't feel right. As he walked back to his car, Jules tried to forget about the random encounters but his mind kept drifting back to the roller rink.

He was great sex. Yes, but I don't want to get involved with anyone. Yeah, but maybe we could just play once more. Why not go for someone new? There's plenty more cocks in the barn...erggh I sound like Jock.

On Friday morning, Jules found himself standing before an azure-blue, metal door with his toolbox in hand. He'd been called out to repair a malfunctioning shower and was about to knock when the door was suddenly opened to reveal none other but Cain, wearing a skimpy pair of white running shorts and a loose red singlet that exposed the sides of his taunt torso.

Seriously? Damn he looks even hotter.

"Oh! I was just coming out to get the mail," explained Cain, before apparently taking note of Jules' green polo, which bore the insignia of his handyman business. "You're the repair guy? Jules, right?"

"Yes, and it's Cain?"

"Sure is."

"Sorry, I didn't realize it was you with the order...I didn't know your last name."

"And here I was beginning to think you were stalking me."

"Hardly," scoffed Jules. "Oh, sorry, that came out a bit harsher than I planned."

"No problem. At least I know how you are with handling pipes."

"I do my best."

The undercurrent of sexual tension between them was unmistakable. If he weren't there on professional reasons, Jules would've already made a move and undoubtedly be plowing Cain senseless on the carpeted floor of the hallway.

"So, did you enjoy your treatment?" inquired Cain, a curious smile visiting his lips.

"Sorry?"

"At L'Hommerie."

"Oh...yeah, it was really good actually. I hadn't been there before."

"Yes, I know." Seeing Jules' quizzical expression Cain elaborated. "I'm the owner and I *definitely* would've remembered if you'd been in before."

Given Cain's tone, Jules had an inkling that he'd be doing a bit more customer service than he'd planned. Following Cain down the hallway, Jules noted a number of photos framed on the walls, featuring Cain posing with an identical looking man. He paused, a tad astonished.

"You're a twin?" asked Jules, gesturing to the nearest photo of them wearing exceedingly brief Speedos at a beach.

"Yeah, that's my brother Abel." Before Jules could even comment Cain continued. "And yes, our parents have a twisted sense of humor."

"Sorry, I was just a bit surprised. I'm actually a triplet and one of my brothers married a twin too."

"Is that a proposal?" quipped Cain, mischief in his eyes.

"We should see how the repair goes first."

Cain's face broke out into a broad grin, obviously pleased with Jules' sense of humor.

"Yes, true. I wouldn't want to marry a man without testing out all of his skills."

The heavy flirting sparked a stirring in Jules' underwear but he decided that it would be best for Cain to make the first move, given the circumstances. Unhappily for Jules' crotch, it appeared as if Cain planned on drawing the proceedings out further. Leading the way, Cain directed Jules up the stairs to the first floor. The view of Cain's posterior straining against the flimsy material of his running shorts ensured that Jules' crotch began to bulge with need.

"Here you go," said Cain, gesturing through the open door of the bathroom. "I'll be just pottering about the house, let me know if you need anything?"

"Will do."

Setting to work immediately, Jules soon found the source of the problem, a blocked pipe that didn't need too much unclogging. Around an hour later, Jules screwed the taps back into place and tested the water flow.

Fantastic.

Walking out to the landing Jules called out to Cain, who appeared from his bedroom at the end of the hallway. He padded down the hallway and watched in an interested manner as Jules demonstrated the fixed shower.

"Perfect!" declared Cain. "Now that that's out of the way. How about we test out your handiwork?"

Without waiting for a response, Cain moved forward and wrapped Jules up in a tight embrace, kissing him hard upon the lips. The pair quickly disrobed then Cain pulled Jules back into the newly fixed shower and turned it on. The water cascaded over their undulating bodies, as the bathroom filled with steam. Their tongues dueled together and the clearly aroused manhoods rubbed together in anticipation.

Skipping the foreplay, Cain quickly jumped out to retrieve some condoms from the bathroom cabinet and then lubed himself up with lotion. He braced himself against the aqua-colored tiled wall as Jules donned his protection before aiming his weapon at the target and firing home.

Unlike their hurried first encounter, Jules had nowhere to be for a few hours so was more than happy to take his time properly exploring Cain's insides. He slid his cock in and out of the tight tunnel with slow, purposeful movements, as he bit the back of Cain's neck and ran his hands all over the slippery torso in front of him. Jules admired the visual contrast of his pale skin rubbing up against Cain's darker hue.

After nearly half an hour, Jules was feeling slightly waterlogged and decided that it was time to wrap things up. Jules began to hammer away, his hips bouncing off of Cain's beautiful buttocks. Their mutual moaning echoed around the tiled space and mingled with the sound of skin slapping together at a furious pace. Before too long, his cock throbbed and Jules clutched onto Cain with a vice-like grip, as he pumped his seed into the latex sheath. Reaching around, Jules gave Cain's member a handful of strokes, which triggered him to spurt his load all over the tiles in front of him.

Turning around, Cain's face was the very picture of contentment. He gave Jules a rather tender kiss. Looking down, he then raised his hand to take a hold of the circular amulet hanging on a thin chain around Jules' neck. It appeared to be made of very old silver and was covered in engravings with a J in the center.

"I like your pendant," murmured Cain. "Very unusual looking."

"Thanks, it's a family heirloom." In turn, Jules noticed Cain's necklace. "I like yours too. Whalebone?"

"Yeah, it was a present from an ex. Apparently it absorbs part of the life force of whoever wears it…if you believe in that kind of thing. It's certainly had enough cum spilt on it over the years," laughed Cain. "Anyway, enough about jewelry, we should definitely do this again."

My thoughts exactly…

"Right now?" asked Jules, his manhood twitching at the prospect.

"Mmm, sure," agreed Cain, pushing his nakedness harder against Jules. "But I meant I'd be fun to play again on another day too."

"I'd like that."

Turning off the water, the pair climbed out and Cain handed Jules an over-sized, fluffy white towel to dry himself off.

"If you don't have to rush, my bed is pretty comfortable," offered Cain grinning.

"Yes, it might be nice to lie down for a little while. And maybe we can add some life force to that necklace of yours."

"And I want a chance at that ass," declared Cain, slapping Jules on the buttocks.

"Maybe if you're a good boy."

"Never!"

Grabbing Jules' hand, Cain led the handyman down the hall and soon the towels were thrown to the floor and their sport began anew.

Two hours later, Jules left the townhouse and could feel himself beaming.

Good to have a new fuckbuddy...now maybe I'll stop playing with...nope, not even going to think about him.

* * *

Over the next month, Jules and Cain caught up on a weekly basis. Nothing romantic mind you, just good old-fashioned fucking, although sometimes they lingered afterwards and chatted amiably in the afterglow. It had been difficult at times for Jules to stick to his strict policy of no sleepovers, as the conversation and the bed had become increasingly comfortable.

He's human, I can't. Even if he wasn't I shouldn't get involved. I'm not ready for anything serious. It's been five years, when will I be ready?

Returning home from one such afternoon tryst, Jules was in a thoroughly good mood. The pair had engaged in a delightful spot of light bondage, which had left several marks of Cain upon his skin. His contentment quickly evaporated, however, when he pulled into his driveway and saw an unwelcome visitor standing on his front porch – his ex, Harrison.

What the hell is he doing here? I know why he's here, there's no use pretending.

As he got out of his van and approached the porch, Jules felt his pulse quicken and a stirring in his pants. The response was a completely involuntary one as it was the effect that Harrison and his kind had over others – both human and supernatural alike. It was one of the reasons that it had been so hard to leave him.

Fucking fairies.

"What are you doing here, Harry?" growled Jules irritably.

"Well, what kind of greeting is that?" asked Harrison with a demure smile.

Paying no attention to his ex's obvious attitude, Harrison moved forward and gave Jules a gentle kiss. It tingled on his lips and sent little electric shocks down towards his crotch, which began to bulge indecently despite himself.

Dammit!

"What do you want?" demanded Jules, his bad temper growing with each passing moment.

"Who's the guy?" inquired Harrison

"What?"

"Don't play coy, you know I can sense him on you."

"Nobody you know…or need to know."

"Honestly, I don't know what you think of me. I innocently pop by to say hello and you couldn't be frostier."

"What do you expect? I'm not your doormat anymore, Harry."

He turned to go into his house when Harrison stopped him by grabbing his forearm and sent a shiver through his body that awakened his cock fully.

"Harry, no!" shouted Jules.

"Don't be like that. We had fun together, didn't we?"

"That doesn't make up for everything else. You cheated on me, only the gods know how many times, whenever you disappeared for days on end for *fairy business*."

"True, I wasn't the most faithful of partners but must we always dwell on the bad? I always kept you *satisfied*, didn't I? We never had any problems there." To emphasis his point, Harrison moved his right hand down to the extremely noticeable outline of Jules' manhood and gave it a firm squeeze. "And tonight, I was at a bit of a loose end and needed some company. What do you say, help a friend out?"

Despite their sexual powers, fairies still couldn't force people to do anything they didn't already wish to. It was more of a loosening of their target's inhibitions, which made it all that harder for Jules. He loved the sex but wasn't particularly fond of the man – not any more. To be fair, things had been great at the beginning, but Harrison's free and easy nature wasn't conducive to an exclusive long-term relationship. They broke up roughly a dozen times before it finally stuck five years ago. Even now, the longest they'd gone without fucking was about a month. While they seemed to be incapable of having bad sex, Jules always regretted it afterwards.

Say no. Tell him to go to hell. Have some damn self-respect. I just got what I needed from Cain.

"This is the last time," muttered Jules.

"Sure, J. Whatever you say," grinned Harrison in victory.

Minutes later, after a hasty removal of clothing, they were naked in Jules' bed with Harrison's cock wedged firmly inside of Jules' ass. They tended not to bother with foreplay – the first round.

Fuck he still feels so good. I need to stop doing this. It isn't healthy but it feels so fucking good.

Harrison left several hours later, leaving a very sore but sated Jules lying in bed in a tumultuous state of mind.

When will I ever learn?

* * *

Just over a week later, Jules was in the middle of babysitting his nieces, while his brother and Seth had some much-needed alone time. The girls had unanimously decided upon the afternoon activity – a brightly colored cartoon extravaganza that Jules knew he was going to hate. Exiting the sunny terrace of One Happy Piggy, the trio had happily demolished a delicious lunch of maple syrup drenched pancakes and chocolate thick-shakes – he tended to spoil them rotten.

Their parents can worry about the vegetables.

They were wandering to the Cineplex down the street when Jules felt a tap on his shoulder. Turning around, he came face-to-face with a delightful surprise.

"Hey, Mister," greeted Cain.

"Hi," said Jules, happy to see Cain but also feeling a tad self-conscious in front of his nieces.

"And are these young ladies yours?" asked Cain, turning on the charm.

"No, he's ours," interjected Amy.

"I see."

"Who do you belong to?" added Isabelle.

"That's still up for grabs," declared Cain, with a wide friendly grin. "Precocious, aren't they?"

"You don't know the half of it. These sweet young things are my nieces, Amy and Isabelle. Girls, this is Cain."

"Is he your boyfriend, Uncle Jules?" asked Amy.

"Ah…no."

"Why not? Don't you want him to be?" inquired Isabelle.

"No, it's not like…"

"We heard Daddy telling Papa that you need a boyfriend so that you can finally forget about the mean fairy," added Amy.

"Did he just?" remarked Cain, looking thoroughly bemused.

"But I thought all fairies were nice and good," chimed in Isabelle.

"Not all of them," muttered Jules. "Listen girls, Cain and I are just friends. OK?"

"Yes, Uncle Jules," they chorused.

Feeling decidedly mortified, Jules turned back to Cain and gave an apologetic shrug.

"Sorry, about that."

"Nah, it's fine. They're cute. Reminds me of how me and my brother were at that age. Absolute angels."

"Ha! I doubt that," scoffed Jules.

An awkward pause followed, as neither Jules nor Cain seemed to know quite how to act with one another in front of their captive audience. The uncomfortable silence was soon broken by yet another question.

"Did you want to join us, Cain?" offered Amy.

"We're seeing The Emoji Movie sequel," exclaimed Isabelle excitedly.

At this point, Jules was half-hoping for his nieces to magically lose their voices.

This is so embarrassing. I doubt he'll want to hook up again after being bombarded by the girls. If only I didn't love them so much.

"Sure, why not," agreed Cain, to Jules' great surprise.

"Are you sure? You really don't have to."

"Nah, I've really been wanting to see it." Cain's sly smile betrayed the truth. "Lead the way!"

And so, the foursome made their way down the street and soon found themselves seated in the front row, laden down with an inordinate amount of popcorn, candy and soda, surrounded by a worrying number of noisy youngsters.

Apparently in matchmaking mode, the girls had forced Jules and Cain to sit side by side. During the film their legs brushed up against each other and Jules found his thoughts turning rather carnal in nature. This only increased when their fingers brushed up against one another when they'd both gone for some popcorn. After the second time, their fingers lingered, intertwining in amongst the salty-buttery goodness. Fortunately, the presence of the girls – and the cinema full of people – kept things from becoming too heated. Jules kept sneaking side-glances at Cain, who was doing the same, especially when there'd been a particularly corny scene.

This is kinda nice though. Maybe there could be more with him than just hot sex.

As they walked back into the bright sunshine of the late August day, Jules was seized by an unexpected impulse.

"We're planning on going for ice cream before I drop the girls home. I really like to load them up with sugar before I return them," confessed Jules, with a hint of maliciousness. "You're welcome to join us, if we haven't already bored you senseless that is?"

"Not even close," declared Cain. "I'd love to tag along."

The girls squealed their approval and they headed off for their just desserts. Several large sugary helpings later, it was time to part ways. Securing his nieces into the car, Jules turned to say goodbye.

"I had a really nice time this afternoon."

"Me too," replied Cain, moving in closer to Jules. "It was fun."

"Yeah, it was good seeing you in a…different setting. We should do it again sometime. But maybe without the girls."

"That'd be great. So, what are you doing later?"

"Nothing planned," answered Jules

"I wouldn't be opposed to some…*company*."

They were both aware that little ears were probably listening intently to their conversation, so they kept things at a PG level.

"How about I swing by after I've dropped them off. We can start working off that ice cream."

"Sounds good to me."

Fighting the urge to kiss Cain, Jules simply smiled.

"See you in a bit then."

"Goodbye, Uncle Cain!" sang the girls, followed by a great deal of giggling.

Cringing, Jules hopped in the driver's seat. Looking in the side mirror he saw Cain laughing and he didn't feel quite so awkward.

An hour later, Jules knocked on the familiar blue door, which was soon opened by a completely naked Cain, who dragged him inside and welcomed him with an eager kiss.

"What if it hadn't been me?" inquired Jules when they broke for air.

"Then whoever it was would've gotten a nice surprise."

They resumed their frantic kissing and made it as far as the plush, carpeted lounge room floor before their animalistic needs fully took hold. After Cain disrobed Jules, they fell into a hungry sixty-nine, which was followed by equally as ravenous rimming and then a good deal of fucking. By the time they were finished it was around one in the morning. They were lying in Cain's king-sized bed, having finally made it to the bedroom after round two.

"Did you want to stay over?" proposed Cain.

The question put Jules in a thoroughly conflicted state of mind. He was tired and it felt very nice to be holding Cain's naked body next to his, but his emotional baggage still weighed heavy upon him.

Am I ready for this? It's just for one night. It doesn't have to mean anything. Yeah, but it does and...maybe I want it to.

"I...sure, why not."

"Great! I didn't feel like getting up to let you out," admitted Cain.

"Ah, I feel so welcome."

"After what we've just been doing all evening you'd damn well better."

"I do, I do," assured Jules, as he gave Cain's neck and face a series of tender kisses.

Snuggling in closer together, Jules felt a warm wave of contentment flow through his body.

I'd forgotten how good this feels. Maybe dating a human wouldn't be the worst thing.

* * *

A month passed and Jules was definitely smitten. He and Cain saw each other most days and there'd been quite a few sleepovers. Neither of them had broached the 'are we boyfriends?'

conversation but it was clearly a direction they were heading in. For his part, Jules had stopped seeking satisfaction in the arms of other men, happy to let Cain see to his carnal needs. In a great show of fortitude, he'd resisted temptation and turned down a late-night visit from Harrison, who was most unimpressed at being rejected.

"You'll change your mind," jeered Harrison. "I know how to give you what you *need*."

Ignoring Harrison's taunts, Jules kept happily returning to Cain's welcoming embrace. Their sex had only gone from strength to strength with Jules feeling more fulfilled and content than he had for a long time.

Unfortunately, there was a slight problem closer to home in the form of his brother. Jock seemed disappointed by the developing relationship and made no secret of his thoughts on the matter.

"I don't know why you're bothering with him," remarked Jock dismissively, as they were unloading supplies into their garage from the white work van. "Isn't one human in the family enough?"

"I'm sure that's *speciesist*. Anyway, it worked out fine for Jasper and you like Seth, don't you?"

"You know I do, but it's just easier to play with our own kind. I mean have you even told him what you are?"

"No, I haven't found the right time."

"You'd better tell him before Halloween. You don't want him finding out by accident like Seth did."

Their brother-in-law had stumbled upon their supernatural secret quite a few years ago, when he'd interrupted one of their most sacred rituals. It had nearly ended the relationship between

Jasper and Seth, but luckily, they'd been able to overcome their trust issues and work things out.

"Why do you care anyway?" growled Jules, annoyed by having to justify his actions.

"I don't see why you're all so damn desperate to leave me."

"What are you talking about? We're still in the same city and we see each other all the time."

"I just want it to be like how it used to be. Us all living together and having fun."

"We did that for over a century, besides I'm not moving out again any time soon. Cain and I are just dating, who knows where it's heading. I really don't understand why you're being like this."

"I...I don't want to end up alone," admitted Jock in a rare show of vulnerability.

Of the three brothers he was always the most closely guarded with his feelings. So much so that Jules and Jasper often joked the only ones he had were restricted purely to his erogenous zones.

I knew he was a big softie.

"You'll always have us," reassured Jules. "We aren't going anywhere."

"You say that but Jasper's already going to die before us because he's been giving Seth his essence. Now you're with a human and will probably end up doing the same. Can't you just be happy with random sex and no commitment like you were before?"

"But I wasn't happy, Jock, not really. It's why I kept fucking around with Harrison because I never really got over him...until now. That only happened because I'm trying to open up my heart to someone new. You love Seth and the girls. Don't I deserve the same shot at happiness? Don't you?"

"I don't want kids," grumbled Jock, but there was a tiny softening in his tone. "The idea of settling down turns my stomach, but if that's what you want to do I don't see how I can stop you."

"Awww, you're getting soft in your old age," mocked Jules cheerfully.

"I'll give you soft!"

With that Jock knocked Jules to the ground and the pair began to wrestle right there on the driveway, acting like the little boys they once were. They rolled around laughing and grunting in a most immature display of brotherly affection.

Fifteen minutes later they were both lying panting on the floor having proved an equal match for one another.

"We OK?" asked Jules. "No more mean remarks about Cain?"

"Yeah, I guess."

"OK, good. Let's finish unloading this stuff. I need to have a shower before I go see Cain."

They finished the task in companionable silence but Jules had a lot on his mind. As much as it pained him to admit it, Jock was right. While he wasn't sure where things would end up with Cain, Jasper knew that he was well past caring for him in a purely physical sense.

If I do want a future with him, he needs to know, especially with Halloween coming. He'll either think I'm crazy or...I don't know what he's going to think. Seth handled it OK...eventually. Maybe Cain will, too.

A few weeks went by and Jules had debated the pros and cons of telling Cain the truth about his family every day. He'd come close to saying something a few times but his fear overrode his better judgment. Halloween was fast approaching and Jules knew he was running out of time.

Lying in bed after a particularly energetic fuck, Jules decided to bite the bullet and come out of the supernatural closet.

"So, I need to tell you something," began Jules nervously.

"Oh, honey!" cried Cain, laughing. "Yes, I want to get married and have a whole minivan full of babies, too!"

"You're an idiot."

"Hey!" shouted Cain sitting up, in mock outrage. "Well, if that's your attitude, don't think this will be getting any more attention from me."

He playfully tapped Jules' manhood and poked out his tongue.

"Now, now. No need to be like that," placated Jules, giving Cain some gentle kisses. "I'm sure we can work something out."

"Maybe," conceded Cain, as he surrendered to Jules' lips. "OK, what did you want to tell me?"

"It's…um…well, it's…about me…and my family as well."

Turning to face Jules, Cain had a knowing look on his face.

"I know that you guys aren't exactly regular. So what type of supers are you?"

What? How could he? This was so not what I expected.

"We're…umm…guardian angels, but how did you know?"

"Come on, I'm not stupid. There've been lots of little things, but the biggest clue was that photo in your lounge room of you and your brothers at Woodstock. So, unless you all have incredibly good surgeons, you're a lot older than you look."

"Oh, um, well, that makes sense." Feeling quite silly at their apparent lack of discretion, Jules felt himself smile at the weight lifted. "Do you want to know my real age?"

"Sure."

"Three hundred and forty-two," admitted Jules sheepishly.

"But you don't even look a day over two hundred."

He punched Cain lightly on the arm before giving him a loving peck on the cheek.

"Besides, you aren't exactly my first brush with the otherworldly," added Cain.

"I'm not?"

"No, my brother dated a fairy for a while."

It couldn't be.

"Not Harrison?" asked Jules hesitantly, already fairly sure of the answer.

"Yeah, how did you know?"

The world is too fucking small.

"He...ah..."

"Ahhh, he's the bad fairy your nieces were talking about. If it's any consolation I never really liked him."

"It is."

"Are you still in love with him?"

"NO! It's just that he left me with quite a bit of baggage."

"We all have baggage. I don't care about your past and as long as you keep fucking me the way you do I won't have a problem at all."

"Sounds like a solid plan to me."

They started kissing again and it looked like another round of play was on the cards, when Cain unexpectedly pulled away.

"So...O'Lantern? I'm guessing a descendant of Jack."

"Yup, that'd be Grandpa."

"Ahhh, Pumpkin Boy."

"Not funny," objected Jules without a great deal of conviction.

"Kinda is." Suddenly, Cain got a serious expression on his face. "Since you came out to me, I'm guessing that you trust me."

"I do."

"Does that mean we're boyfriends now?"

Does it? What am I waiting for?

"Would that be OK with you if we were?" asked Jules, a tad uncertainly.

"More than OK."

To emphasize his point, Cain jumped on top of his boyfriend and began to show Jules just how happy he was in the official declaration of their relationship status. The twosome soon became lost in their private little world of loving pleasure.

* * *

Now that the secret was out, Jules was free to reveal to Cain their most sacred duty of the year – the All Hallow's Eve Crossover.

"At Halloween the veil between the living world and the spirit realm is at its weakest and it's the easiest time for us to help lost souls pass to the other side. Together, my brothers and I are able to open a portal to allow the spirits to move on. This time it coincides with a Blood Moon, it's been over a century since they've synced up. Together, it'll ramp up the power substantially and should allow us to create a huge gateway."

"Where do you do it?" inquired Cain, his curiosity evident.

"At Sanctuary."

"The gay club? Isn't that a bit public?"

"No, we do it in a small antechamber in the basement off of the former crypt. The fact that it's a deconsecrated cathedral helps act as a beacon to the lost souls. It's where we've done it for over a century now. We are able to channel and amplify sexual energy to open the portal and the Halloween party they hold certainly ensures that...especially given all the action that goes on in the crypt."

"Sounds like fun. Can I watch?"

"It wouldn't freak you out?"

"Nah, I love all that spooky stuff."

"I'll have to ask my brothers but I don't see why not."

Fortunately, Jock and Jasper had no issue with Cain attending, in fact, Seth decided he wanted to come along as well, so it would be a family affair, their daughters being babysat for the evening.

The fated evening arrived two weeks later and the fivesome arrived at the club together. Jules and Cain were costumed as an angel and a demon, while Jasper and Seth had chosen to go dressed as Batman and Robin, whereas Jock had opted for a Roman gladiator outfit. Naturally, all of their ensembles were carefully chosen to highlight their physical attributes – as was the case for a good many of the other patrons.

The club was packed, as usual, and full to the brim with costumed revelers cavorting with one another. The brothers and their escorts happily spent a few hours enjoying the party, drinking and dancing, and generally appreciating the skimpy outfits of the gym-honed partiers around them. Half an hour before midnight, they made their way downstairs to the former crypt, which served as a well-equipped and well-used back room. The crypt was practically throbbing with pleasure, with a chorus of cocking reverberating off of the sandstone walls. The air was heavily scented with the sweat and spent seed of countless men.

Passing the writhing bodies, the group went to the far-left corner where Jock pressed a small angel on a column and a part of the wall rumbled aside to let them into a small anti-chamber. None of the revelers paid them the least bit of attention thanks to a spell cast by a Wiccan friend of Jock's, Alexander Dash. He was a fine figure of a man in his early-forties, with sharp, intelligent features, a shock of auburn hair, cool blue eyes and a penchant for puppy play. Jock and he had a regular arrangement that saw both their kinky desires met.

The brothers moved into the center of the room and formed a small circle.

"You guys should just stand to the side." Jules suggested to Cain and Seth.

"And probably not next to one another if you don't want to end up fucking," warned Jock with a lascivious wink.

"The *energy* can become quite overpowering," confirmed Jasper.

Seth and Cain exchanged looks of equal bemusement and took places on opposite sides of the anti-chamber.

Jules took the amulet off of his neck and held it up as the brothers started to softly chant in an ancient tongue. As they chanted Jules felt the energy seeping in from the crypt next-door and soon thin green streams of light began to make their way into the room, wrapping themselves around Jules and his brothers before being drawn in towards the pendant, which began to spin slowly by itself. The streams began to increase in size and brightness and caused the amulet to levitate. Jules let go of the necklace and the amulet stayed in place, floating in mid-air. Looking across at his brothers, Jules saw that their eyes were shining a brilliant green, as he knew his own would be. The engravings on the amulet were also aglow with the same florescent shade.

It's time.

In unison, the brothers began their traditional call to the poor wandering souls.

"Oh, wayward spirits across the land, heed our call. Take refuge here and let us lead you to the next realm. There is nothing holding you in the world. Be free."

Through the walls, white, flickering figures began to appear, as if an old film was being played. Jules looked towards Cain to see how his boyfriend was coping with this otherworldly experience and was pleased to see a look of astonishment and delight upon Cain's handsome features.

The energy flowed through them and Jules felt his cock become erect with the power. It felt even more powerful than the last Blood Moon and it seemed as if the entire world was pulsing with the energy. The spirits flowed into the room in a huge procession all attracted by the energy, crowding around their small circle, and all attention on the spinning amulet.

In his mind's eye, Jules could see the writhing bodies in the next room, the sexual force burning hot within them. Then he could feel the amulet stretching its reach further, drawing down the essence from the club goers above. From here, his vision expanded outside noting all the sexual energy in the city, from the people pleasuring themselves alone, to the couples...and more. Normally, this would be the extent of the amulet's range, but to his surprise Jules felt it searching outwards through the suburbs and into the countryside, feeding off the various couplings it encountered. At the rate of expansion, Jules feared that they may be losing control of the energy and was about to signal his brothers when all of a sudden there was an almost blindingly white light. In the center of the light appeared two men in the midst of a ferocious union in what looked to be a field. Jules had never seen anything so powerful.

They can't be merely human.

Moments later, the men in his vision climaxed together, their forms looking more bestial by the second. Their combined release sent an enormous surge of energy back towards the city and hurtling towards the amulet. The room began to shake as the raw power flooded into the room and the air around the amulet began to crackle and pop as the very fabric between realms was ripped asunder. The portal sprang into existence and appeared far larger than ever before. A soft white light bathed the brothers in a heavenly glow, as hundreds of souls began to exit the world in a blur before them. Once the room was devoid of spirits the portal closed with a loud crack, releasing the unused sexual energy. It hurtled outwards, hitting the brothers, Cain and Seth, who all orgasmed without touching themselves. The wave of energy continued into the next room where it had a similar effect, causing all the men to ejaculate in unison, their grunts and cries almost deafening as they reverberated against the sandstone walls of the crypt. It continued to flow through the building dissipating as it went so that the patrons upstairs received a pleasant erotic buzz rather than spontaneous orgasm.

"What the hell was that?" exclaimed Jules.

"It was fucking awesome! That's what!" shouted Jock. "Especially whoever it was in that field."

"Werewolves," commented Jasper. Seeing his brothers' confused looks he explained further. "I used to date a were, remember."

"Oh, did you just?" questioned Seth.

"That was..." began Cain, looking rather unsteady on his feet. He hadn't left his post by the wall. "I...um..."

"You OK?" asked Jules, the concern clear in his voice.

Maybe it was all too much.

"Jules, I..."

Suddenly, Cain collapsed to the floor in a heap. The others quickly gather around, Jules taking Cain in his arms. After around five seconds, Cain moaned slightly and lazily opened his eyes as he started to come around.

"Cain, can you hear me?" demanded Jules.

"Yeah," answered Cain, his voice thick with fatigue. "It was just so much."

"Sorry, I forget how intense it can be and tonight was ridiculously powerful. The Blood Moon certainly amped things up. Can you stand?"

"Yeah, I think so."

Jules and Jock helped Cain to his feet. He was a tad wobbly at first but soon regained his balance.

"I think I'd better take you home," recommended Jules.

"As you command, my Angel."

"We're headed home, too" announced Jasper, taking Seth by the hand. "Need to relieve the babysitter."

"I'm not," declared Jock. "I have some energy to burn off."

They left the anti-chamber and walked through the crypt area, where piles of men were just rousing themselves following their exhaustive mutual release. Leaving the group, Jock grabbed the nearest comely muscleman and began to kiss him hard. The man in question wasted no time in reciprocating and soon the pair was pressed up against the wall ravishing one another.

An hour later, Jules and Cain were in bed together cuddling. Cain seemed much more his normal self but still a little tired.

"That was incredible," said Cain. "At the club. Thanks for sharing your world with me."

"My pleasure. I'm glad it didn't freak you out."

"Not at all. It was fun but now I'm exhausted. Time for sleep." As Cain turned over and began to drift off he mumbled. "Love you, Pumpkin Boy."

Jules felt uneasy. It was the first time that Cain had said the L word. The words warmed his heart but he wasn't ready to reciprocate them just yet.

Soon I hope.

Unfortunately, that wasn't the only thing worrying Jules. Despite Cain's protests that he was fine, Jules had a nagging sense that something wasn't quite right. It was a familiar sensation that he'd had before, but he couldn't quite remember when.

Hopefully, it's nothing.

* * *

A few weeks later, the first snow of the season began to fall, turning the cityscape into a pristine magical land – until the cars and citizens began their daily journeys and made a great deal of slush in the process. It also meant that it was time for one of Jules' favorite events – the annual winter carnival held in Janeway Park. Every year, it raised money for a different charity in the city, this year the proceeds were to go towards an equipment upgrade for Picard Children's Hospital.

The experience at Halloween had made the pair closer but Jules still found that as much as he wanted to he couldn't commit himself fully. Indeed, he was yet to utter those three little words that he knew Cain wanted to hear.

Wrapped up warmly in heavy winter coats, the couple walked into the north entrance of the park and was immediately hit by noise, color and movement. All along the wide paths there were a multitude of tents and stalls, advertising games, food and music.

"It gets bigger every year," declared Cain, looking around at all the amusements on offer.

"Let's go spend some bucks for those sick kids then."

Gloved hand in hand they wandered along the path, stopping to grab some mulled wine to warm themselves up on their journey. After a few minutes they came to a stand that had an extremely long line. Looking towards the head of the queue, they could see why. It was called Dunk-a-Dude and the aim of the game was to throw a ball at a metal panel to send a rather buff blond man into the water. He was wearing small electric-blue Speedos, which did nothing to disguise his generous assets. Fortunately, the water was heated, judging by the steam coming up off of it. The sign announced that a local fraternity, Pi Alpha Pi, was behind the game. Off to the side of the tank there were about ten other lads with white terry toweling robes on, obviously waiting for their turn to be dunked.

"Wanna have a go?" asked Cain, with a mischievous look in his eyes. "It is for a good cause, after all."

"Nothing at all to do with seeing slippery frat boys, I'm sure."

They patiently waited their turn and fifteen minutes later it was time to show off their ball throwing skills. While Cain missed on his first two attempts, his third hit the mark and sent an auburn-haired man into the tank. The dunked dude then hopped out of the tank and was quickly enveloped by his fellow frat brothers, who were on hand with towels to get him warmed up again, although it's be fair to say a good many of the people watching would've eagerly volunteered to help given the chance – Jules and Cain among them. Jules then had his go and sent a good-looking Latino lad tumbling into the water on his first try. There were a few gasps among the gathered crowd when the lad in question got out of the tank and the almost unbelievable length of his member was seen in the now see-thru white swimwear.

The gods were certainly generous to him.

After wandering around for another hour and playing various games – Cain won a fluffy pink teddy bear at the shooting gallery, which he'd promptly gifted to Jules – they came across a fortuneteller tent at the far end of the fair. There was a hand painted sign out the front proclaiming the services offered by Madame Gabriella.

"Come on, she reads palms," announced Cain, with a touch of childish glee. "It'll be fun."

"She's probably a fraud. I'm surprised she doesn't read tealeaves too," taunted Jules.

"Come on, where's your sense of adventure. Besides I thought someone of your heritage would be more open-minded."

"I am, but the truly gifted psychics don't tend to have tents at fundraisers."

Entering the tent, they found a woman in her mid-fifties, with frizzy curly brunette hair and wide kind brown eyes, and costumed, as one would imagine a carnival fortuneteller. Upon her fingers there were abundance of rings and her flowing gypsy-style dress was adorned with brightly colored, silk scarves.

"Oh, such a handsome couple, I see your auras are practically the same shade, very in sync indeed. Come let me tell your fortunes," beseeched Madame Gabriella.

They sat down on the wooden chairs in front of her small round table, which held a stack of Tarot cards.

"You first," nudged Jules.

Barely controlling his urge to smirk, Jules watched as Cain offered up his hand for inspection.

"Let's see what we have here," murmured Madame Gabriella.

"Am I going to rich and famous and have a string of lovers around the world?" questioned Cain, a naughty smile upon his face.

"Is that what you really want then, is it?" asked Jules, with an air of mock-offence.

"I'd have you there, too...if you're a good boy."

"Ha. You first."

It was then that Jules realized that the fortuneteller was frowning and her brown eyes had taken on a watery aspect. A strange unsettled feeling ran through Jules, his senses feeling heightened.

"I'm so sorry, dearie," she whispered.

"What?" demanded Cain urgently. "What did you see?"

"That you'll die of a broken heart before the year is out. I'm ever so sorry. There's no charge for the..."

Cain fled the tent before she'd even finished and was swiftly followed by Jules, leaving a very forlorn looking Gabriella sitting quite still.

Jules caught up with him just before Cain reached the south gates of the park.

"Cain, wait up!"

Grabbing a hold of him, Jules span his boyfriend around to see that his eyes were stained with tears.

"Cain, what is it? You don't actually believe that old biddy do you?"

"But, she...she's right," lamented Cain, the tears now falling freely. "I am going to die of a broken heart."

"You're not making any sense."

"I was born with a degenerative heart condition and it will most likely kill me. It runs in our family and it killed my granddad and uncle. Fortunately, it missed Abel...I wasn't so lucky. But I've never let it define my life. I've always tried to live as fully as I can. God, now I sound like one of those awful inspirational quotes."

Jules now remembered why he'd been unsettled by the niggling feeling he'd had ever since Halloween and that he'd been doing his level best to ignore. He'd experienced it some two hundred years before, when death was near at hand, at the time of his own grandparents passing.

He should've told me!

"Why didn't you say anything?" asked Jules, trying to keep calm.

"I was planning on telling you, but...I...I didn't want to lose you. So, this is your out, if you want it. It's been a deal breaker for guys in the past, which is why I don't tend to tell anyone until it gets really serious."

"Is that why you collapsed at Halloween?"

"Yes," admitted Cain reluctantly. "I saw my cardiologist a few days later. The rate of deterioration has progressed faster than they'd hoped. My valves are losing strength, which is screwing with my blood pressure. Without a heart replacement I may only have another year at most. The waiting lists are ridiculously long so the chances of a match being found in time are slim at best."

Of course, I get involved with the one human that has an even shorter lifespan. I wish there was something I could do. There is something...don't be a coward.

Coming to a decision, Jules took Cain into his arms and hugged him tightly.

"You're going to have to try harder than that to get rid of me. I'm not going anywhere," whispered Jules. "I love you."

Their lips locked in a passionate kiss by the gates, the noise of the fair fading away as they were briefly ensconced in their own little bubble. Jules wished he could freeze time and leave them safe in that moment for forever, but sadly he knew that nobody had that kind of power.

What's the point of my gifts if I can't use them to help the man I love?

* * *

Several weeks passed and it appeared as if luck might be on their side. It was the last day of the year and Cain hadn't had any further incidents. While they'd talked about Cain's condition since that night in the park, neither of them had brought up the psychic's prediction, although it had been at the forefront of Jules' thoughts.

After cleaning the house in preparation for the New Year's Eve party they were hosting, Jules and Cain were in the former's bedroom getting dressed.

"Looks like Madame Gabriella was wrong," asserted Cain smugly. "I'm still here."

Coming behind his boyfriend, Jules gave Cain a big hug and kissed the side of his neck.

"I wish there was something I could do."

"You're doing it just by being here with me and being your lovable self. It makes me appreciate our time together more. Anyway, enough of that, it's a night to celebrate."

The guests began to arrive around nine in the evening and an hour later the place was busy with revelers. Merry conversation flowed throughout the house, as the guests became increasingly inebriated. As it neared midnight, Jules and Cain were chatting happily with some friends in the lounge room when an unexpected guest joined their group.

"Why are you here?" demanded Jules, in his most impolite tone.

"And a happy new year to you too, J," drawled Harrison. Turning his attentions to Cain he smiled wickedly. "Such a delight to see you again, Cain. How's your brother?"

"Fine, he's living in Berlin with his husband," remarked Cain, barely concealing his displeasure.

"Off the market, what a shame."

"You didn't answer me," insisted Jules. "Why are you at our party?"

"Ask Jock," answered Harrison, a trace of spite his tone. "He's the one that invited me."

"But why would he?" An unpleasant reality dawned on Jules. "You mean that…you and he are?"

"Don't look so shocked. You weren't around to play with any more so I found the next best thing. See you next year."

He sauntered off leaving a glowering Jules in his wake.

"I can't believe Jock would be so selfish and unthinking to date Harrison."

"If it's any consolation, I doubt there's anything more going on than an exchange of bodily fluids," soothed Cain.

"Nope, doesn't help. How about we go upstairs to my room and play around instead?"

"Whatever helps you get through it, Pumpkin Boy."

"When are you going to quit it with that nickname?" Jules sighed with only a slight mock exasperation.

"Never!"

After several minutes of making out in his bedroom, Jules was in a much better mood. Noticing the time, Jules took Cain up to the small terrace on the roof to look out over the twinkling lights of the surrounding suburbs, as he wanted to be alone with him.

As they walked outside, rugged up against the cold, a light snow began to fall upon them.

"It's beautiful, out here," declared Cain. "I'm so happy to be here with you."

"Me too."

They could hear the music switched off downstairs as the guests prepared to countdown into the New Year. As the partiers began to chant the descending numbers, Jules turned to Cain but was disturbed to see his boyfriend with a pained expression on his face.

"Cain, what is it?"

"I...I don't feel..." He collapsed to the ground, the color draining from his face. "I'm sorry, Pumpkin Boy."

"Five, four, three..." came the disembodied voices from downstairs.

"Cain! Cain, no you can't go. We haven't had enough time."

Grabbing his amulet from under his shirt he placed it against Cain's heart, trying to channel its energy. The engravings began to glow slightly before fading away again. Cain's eyelids fluttered briefly before coming to a rest and he stopped breathing.

"NO! Dammit, I can't lose him!"

Using the telepathic link to his brothers, Jules screamed for help. Within thirty seconds his brothers burst onto the terrace with Seth and Harrison in tow.

"Why did you bring him?" yelled Jules, upon seeing Harrison

"I thought he could help," explained Jock with an apologetic expression.

"Can you, Harry? Can you help me fix this?" begged Jules, his voice cracking with emotion. "There isn't enough power left in the amulet. Can you bring him back? You owe me!"

"I don't have that kind of power," admitted Harrison forlornly. All of a sudden, his eyes lit up with an idea. "But I may know someone who does."

"Who? Can they get here in time?"

"Yes, but he probably won't do it without a hefty price," warned Harrison. "Are you sure?"

"I don't care, I'd give anything to get him back."

"OK. It's your life." Retrieving his phone from his front pocket, Harrison hit number two on his speed dial. "Hi Luc, It's Harry. Yeah, I know it's been a while but I could really use a favor. OK, then. Thanks."

"Well?" demanded Jules.

"He'll be right here."

"Whe…"

A bright red flash lit up the terrace and there before them stood a handsome man with raven hair, emerald eyes, a ridiculously ripped body and a definite aura of dangerous temptation about him. The fact that he was wearing a black PVC jockstrap and thigh-high leather boots, only added to the appeal.

"Lucifer Morningstar, at your service," proclaimed the man, a lustful twinkle in his eyes.

"You know the fucking Devil?" screeched Jules, feeling increasingly desperate.

"We kinda dated, after you and I broke up," justified Harrison. "I mean look at him, how could I not?"

"Boys, I hate to interrupt," stated Lucifer. "But there's an orgy I really need to get back to."

"Yes, of course. I'm sorry. It's my boyfriend. His heart gave out and he just…died! Can you please bring him back?" begged Jules.

"Ah, dead body. Yes, I can see how that would put a cramp in your evening. That is a big ask, my dear, and will require a grand sacrifice."

"ANYTHING!"

"Are you prepared to give up your supernatural life?" asked Lucifer. "To become fully human?"

"I am," stated Jules without hesitation. "I don't want to live without him by my side."

"Alright then, let me see. We can use that amulet of yours and…his whalebone necklace. The two together should act as a conduit to transfer the energy. Place your hand on his necklace."

Following instructions, Jules placed his hand over the necklace that was lying on top of Cain's still chest.

"WAIT!" cried Jock.

"Please don't try and stop me," begged Jules. "I need to do this."

"I don't want to stop you, idiot. I want to help you." Turning to Lucifer, Jock asked. "If we both gave of our life force would that still leave us as we are?"

"Yes, if you both transferred your essence then you should retain enough to keep you both in your supernatural state, although your lifespans will be significantly decreased."

"I can't ask you to do that," protested Jules.

"You didn't ask. I'm offering. Besides, if you and Jasper are aging faster it means you're going to leave me and as much as you both annoy the bejeezus out of me at times, I don't want to be without you."

"As touching as this all is, the matter is somewhat time sensitive," reminded Lucifer. "Unless you've changed your minds."

"NO!" cried Jules and Jock in unison.

"Alright then, place your hands on the necklace," commanded Lucifer.

A sudden wind swept around the terrace as Lucifer's eyes glowed a dazzling red and the brothers' eyes shone bright green. The effect was immediate and Jules felt the draining of his energy making him weary and he saw Jock being affected the same way. Within seconds, the color slowly returned to Cain's face.

"That should do it," stated Lucifer, matter-of-factly.

With a huge gasp, Cain sat bolt upright breaking the connection between the three of them.

"What's happening?" he asked in a weak voice.

Without answering, Jules pulled Cain into his arms and hugged his boyfriend tight.

"Easy now," objected Cain. "I need to breathe."

"Well, my work here is done," proclaimed Lucifer. "You won't need to worry about his heart any time soon."

Releasing his boyfriend, Jules stood up and gave Lucifer a big bear hug as well.

"I don't know how to thank you," gushed Jules. "I'm forever in your debt, Lucifer."

Something I never thought I'd be saying.

"Handing over you firstborn will be payment enough." Seeing the horrified reaction of all those on the terrace, Lucifer laughed heartily. "Kidding! No sense of humor, honestly. Anyway, you gentlemen aren't the only ones in desperate need of my services. Ciao!"

In a red flash he was gone. Jules hastily turned his attention back to his resurrected lover.

"I thought I'd lost you. Don't ever scare me like that again!"

"But how? Who was that guy? Was I really dead? I don't really remember anything. Shouldn't I have turned into a ghost?"

"Hey, take it easy. Don't worry about any of that right now. I promise I'll answer all your questions later but for now, how about we just spend the rest of the night cuddled up in bed?"

"No objections here," grinned Cain.

Turning to his brother, Jules was filled with gratitude.

"I can never thank you enough."

"Don't worry, I like you owing me," taunted Jock.

"Jerk," said Jules giving his brother a playful swat. "Love you, too. And I may just forgive you for hooking up with Harrison."

"Hey," interjected Harrison. "Seeing as I just helped save your boyfriend's life, I think you should probably cut me and your brother some slack."

"Fine, you're right. I'm sorry. I am truly grateful to both of you."

"Me too," added Cain. "I think...I'm still not quite sure what happened."

"I'm prepared to let bygones be bygones," admitted Jules. "None of that matters anymore."

To prove his point, he gave Harrison a heartfelt hug before returning to his boyfriend's side.

"Now, if you don't mind. I think Cain and I could do with some private time."

The group dispersed and Jules and Cain retired to Jules' bedroom, both understandably weary from the night's events. Stripping off and climbing into bed, the couple then spent a good while kissing and holding one another before both drifting off into a blissful slumber, their worries about their future together banished.

* * *

Thirteen years later, Jules was frozen to the spot with a myriad of emotions swirling through his heart – terror chief among them.

It's too soon. I'm not ready to say goodbye. Where did the time go?

"I don't think I can do this," lamented Jules quietly, afraid of being overheard.

"I don't like it any more than you do, but it's time," whispered Cain, giving his husband's hand a reassuring squeeze.

"Fine. But I'm going to need a big hug afterwards."

"Any time," smiled Cain, the affection clear in his voice. "Ready?"

"No. But it's not like I have a choice."

Turning around in his seat, Jules looked at his five-year-old sons and gave them his best encouraging smile.

"OK, boys. Are you ready for your first day of school?"

"Yes, Daddy," replied Adam, Byron and Caleb in a sing-song manner, their little faces aglow with excitement.

"Alright, then, kiddos. Let's go!" instructed Cain, getting out of the minivan and opening the side door.

Reluctantly joining them, Jules tired his best to keep a calm façade as they walked together towards the school gate. They'd both taken the day off for this very special occasion. Jules knew he would find it hard to concentrate until the boys were all home again. Of course, they'd been to pre-school and had babysitters but this was the first time they'd be gone for the full day and it felt like they were growing up so fast.

Too damn fast!

A minute later, they were at the point of no return and it was all Jules could do not to cry. Looking at his husband, he saw a slightly pained expression and was somewhat relieved.

At least I'm not the only one suffering.

"Now, you're going to behave, aren't you?" asked Cain.

"Yes, Papa," answered the triplets in unison.

"Papa and I will be here to pick you up, at three," added Jules. "Be good, now."

A flurry of hugs and kisses ensued and before Jules knew it, his children were running through the gate without a backward glance.

"It'll be fine," comforted Cain, although his eyes were slightly watery. "How about we go home and find some way of distracting each other?"

"What did you have in mind, good Sir?"

"I'll give you a hint…leather harness."

"That'll do it."

Hand in hand, the pair walked back to the minivan and into a new chapter of their life together.

Maybe we should have more kids?

ABOUT THE AUTHOR

Jimi could be considered to be something of a refined blend of Australian/Polish heritage – given his passion for the arts, vodka and BBQs. He now lives in Paris with his wonderfully understanding French husband and cats.

For other of his raunchy ramblings and published work, feel free to browse http://www.jimify.me follow him on Twitter & Instagram @jimifyme or show your devotion at facebook.com/JIMIFY.ME

DIGITAL TITLES BY JIMI GONINAN

For all Jimi's titles please visit his page at lydianpress.com

IN PRINT FROM LYDIAN PRESS

DOM'S DELIGHTS

Come on in and taste the love!

Dom has worked hard pursuing his dreams of delighting the masses with his tasty treats - indeed his cream has been eagerly eaten all about the town. Now he has almost everything he ever dreamed of – a successful business, loving friends and a beautiful beau. There's just one more thing he needs to make his life complete...to finally marry the man of his dreams!

BEST SERVED HOT

Revenge has never been sweeter.

When Jameson loses everything he holds dear, he almost drowns in a sea of despair. Bitter and broken, he shuns his friends and retreats from the world. Then a chance encounter with a handsome young man offers him a glimmer of hope, and he slowly begins to piece his life back together. Will he be given the second chance at the love he so desperately deserves?

A MAN FOR EVERY OCCASION

There's always time for love.

The bustling city of Port Davinica is home to many stories of love, lust and more than a few happy endings. Follow the adventures of these men as they find love in all manner of places with an amorous touch of the supernatural thrown in for good measure. You'll soon discover in this collection of romantic tales that no matter the festive occasion – Halloween, Christmas, and especially Valentine's Day - there's always time for love.

THE VIRGIN HEART
Some things are worth waiting for.

Abraham Chadwick is locked in a state of quiet desperation. Not only has he never been kissed, he's never even been in love. Indeed, as Abraham prepares for college, he's beginning to fret that he may stay a virgin forever. Fortunately, the sudden arrival of a handsome Southern gentleman into his world gives him a new sense of hope. Will Abraham finally find the love and affection that he's so desired for so long?

THE MILE HIGH CUB
Serviced with a smile!

Time to buckle up it's going to be a bumpy ride… Flying high with Alex Mathieson, who embraces life as an ever-so-friendly air steward with gay abandon. Until, that is, he falls for a handsome pilot, Peter, and a drastic decision sees him heading into unchartered territory, which may change his life forever.

FOUR WEDDINGS AND A SCANDAL!
Here Come the Grooms!

Romance is definitely in the air, as we take the plunge into the sea of matrimony. Get swept up in the excitement, as five very different couples prepare to tie the knot. Not all is as it seems, however, some nasty surprises bring heartache and uncertainty. Will everyone get the happy ending they deserve?

Lydian Press is dedicated to bringing you the finest GLBTQ erotic literature on the web.

Visit us on the web at:

http://lydianpress.com